WILMA STOCKENSTRÖM

The Expedition
to the Baobab Tree

Translated from the Afrikaans by J. M. Coetzee

archipelago books

Published in 2008 by Human & Rousseau, an imprint of NB Publishers,
Cape Town, Africa

First published as *Die Kremetartekspedisie* by Human & Rousseau in 1981.

First Archipelago Books Edition, 2014

Archipelago Books
232 3rd Street #A111
Brooklyn, NY 11215
www.archipelagobooks.org

Library of Congress Cataloging-in-Publication Data
Stockenstrom, Wilma.
[Kremetartekspedisie. English]
The expedition to the baobab tree : a novel / Wilma Stockenstrom ; [translated
by J.M. Coetzee.
pages cm
ISBN 978-1-935744-92-4 (pbk.)
I. Coetzee, J. M., 1940– translator. II. Title.
PT6592.29.T6K713 2014
839.3'635 – dc23

Cover art: Jackson Pollock, *The Moon Woman*

Archipelago gratefully acknowledges the generous support from
Lannan Foundation, the National Endowment for the Arts and the
New York State Council on the Arts, a state agency.

Printed in the United States of America

The Expedition
to the Baobab Tree

WITH BITTERNESS, then. But that I have forbidden myself. With ridicule, then, which is more affable, which keeps itself transparent and could not care less; and like a bird into a nest I can slip back into a tree trunk and laugh to myself. And keep quiet too, perhaps just keep quiet so as to dream outward, for the seventh sense is sleep.

In the past, time often caused trouble when I still wanted to have more than day and night was obsessed with counting and uncertain whether the times during the day when I dozed should be reckoned as night, where night was the eventless and day the busy. Sleep as night. How I sometimes stretched out my nights, curling myself up into the smallest possible bundle in the darkest hollow, forehead pressed against knees to kill the gnawing within myself, entangled in confused thoughts, and fixed on a color to which I held myself so that I could later say, my sleep was blue, or living red like blood, or a grey transitional shade. I woke up crumbled, sat up lightheaded, unsteady, and set a dusty foot down in the great assegai blade of sunlight that bores all day with a steady murderous twist into my dwelling.

That was the time before the beads. The time after the beads can be handled more easily. If I treat myself to sleep so often, it is no longer by chance and for a long while has not been an escape. Then only do I live, I tell myself.

With the beads began my determined effort at dating. I picked them up some days ago, and only later got the idea. I added the new find to the heap of potsherds that curiosity had led me to collect on my trips of varying distances from the tree, hesitant, bored, frustrated trips away from the path to the water that I had by then almost recognizably tramped.

Like the wild animals I make my paths. This conclusion came later. Like the redbuck, no, not like the redbuck and the zebra, not like the buffalo or herd animals of whatever kind that supplement each other's senses and confront crises together and survive what alone they would be too weak for, and that yet fall prey as individuals, and yet die alone, each in his time. I tread my track, so clearly purposeful that I know I have already dwelt a long time in these parts, or rather there has never been any question of dwelling. Rather I should say: I too survive here, but I rely on myself, and even on the days when it feels as if everywhere under the earth there are snake eggs lying, even then I have to fend for myself and try not to tread on them.

My path to the stream, made by me who tread so lightly, thin, faintly winding, weaving past bush and tree trunk and through flat grass plains where the winter is beginning to lie red – my path runs down a final sudden slope to sun-irradiated water wide as my outstretched arms between the trunks of two young matumi trees guarding my drinking place. Further downstream I wash. Higher up, where this tributary debouches into the main stream, is the elephants' ford.

The time when I nearly landed under the feet of the herd, I thought of a riddle that we young girls used to ask each other: What carries its life in its stomach? It must have been all the rumbling bellies that made me giggle anxiously for a moment and then left my throat quite dry in my meager hiding place, with a stone ridge and reeds between them and me. The horde of feet trod springily past me into the pool, the water splashed, they bathed calmly. I shrank into myself. No one grows up under such close protection as a slave girl. I can also add, no one grows up as ignorant as a slave girl, and even I, the shining exception, seem to be stupid when it comes to wild animals and their habits, with my knowledge restricted to items of information about the ivory trade. Every other season an elephant swallows a pebble down, and the pebbles rattle around in their tremendous bellies all their lives, rattle and rattle. Whatever is incomprehensibly huge I reduced to the ridiculous to be able to assimilate it and prove my power over it, while I knelt comically curled up behind stone and reed, a slug without a shell, a soft-shelled beetle as big as the top of my little finger, anxiously in sham death, waiting for the long drawn-out gambols to come to an end so that I could again stand up like a human being and look around. A last trumpeting from the far bank, then I came stiffly erect and brushed the damp sand from me and shivered in the breeze that bent the reeds.

Now I live in friendship with the herd whose ford and bathing place I accidentally trespassed on. Friendship a condescending misnomer, however. I live. They live. Sometimes from my higher ground I see the bent backs milling in the faraway glint of the water, I hear the trumpeting, see pairs of tusks raised momentarily, and still I struggle to make the spectacle cohere with the smooth bracelet that once I could wear. There are connections that evade me.

If I cannot even know everything on the short walk from the entrance to the baobab to the heap of potsherds and other finds, so many steps there, so many back, what of my journey, which sometimes feels as if it took a lifetime and still lasts, still goes on, even if now I am traveling in circles around one place?

So many steps there, with feet already tiring. What did I think I was collecting when I carried it all here . . . ? What did I think I was going to achieve with rubbish . . . ? Time becomes beads and thus rubbish.

On the many paths of my memory there arise threatening figures that block every backward glance. I know these figures. I cannot name them. They loom up before me in the form of something human or sometimes like the corner of a hairy wall or a rolling hut opening that tries to swallow me and drag me off, an opening that storms down in a rage, storms down at a tremendous speed, and then a yard from me suddenly swerves away and saunters and entices me; sometimes too a quiet misshapenness of expectation followed by a noticeable dejection when the multitude of sharp pincers that grip me turn into the slack tendrils of a thicket, when the whole business disappears without further ado leaving an unfathomable grey behind. There are more tracks crisscrossing in my memory than I ever actually saw in a lifetime. What would I not have been able to track down if it had been granted to me and if my detective talent were not so frequently thwarted and the trail petered out inside me?

All kinds of paths leading nowhere radiate from my dwelling. They were not laid on. They came like that. Certainly when I arrived here I used the animal tracks because there was nothing else available except the paths to nowhere, but I soon had to conclude that my way of thinking did not slot in with that of other beings here. And I searched and opened a way and found.

Found, I say. Terrifying.

The most important item, water, I did not have to search for. There is plenty of it. It is visible and audible. I scoop the rippling of the stream up in my gift shell of ostrich egg. I hold the shell in the clear bow of water that leaps over a rough stone so as to catch the light and the sound. Again and again I scoop like this, and pour the water spirit's flickering and murmuring into my gift clay pot. Then I lift the full pot slowly with both hands onto my head, stoop from the knees to pick up my scoop shell, and walk back along the water path to the baobab.

Found: all kinds of veld foods; and found too that I was plucking, digging, picking them up in competition with animals, that trees did not bud and blossom and bear fruit for me to still my hunger, that tubers and roots did not swell underground for me, that not to please me did the greenheart tree drip its nectar, and not to refresh me did the flat crown stand at strategic points in the middle of a patch of shade, and not to give me pleasure did the flecked orchids display themselves, not for me did the violet tree put up tents of scent in early summer.

After the warthogs have grazed, a novice combs the patch of veld where experts have rooted, she kneels like them, tries to pierce the hard ground with a stick where she lacks tusks, tries using her eyesight to search out where she is not endowed with a sense of smell attuned to edible bulbs and roots, and dejectedly comes away with no more than a handful. After the baboons have grazed, the same procedure, except that she makes quite sure that they are out of the way before she ventures onto their terrain.

I fear the baboon's grimace more than the tusks of warthog and bushpig. He is too much like me. I fear my recognizable self in his ugly face. I am reminded of my inferior position here, my lesser knowledge. I feel taunted by the mirroring of my moods and desires in his monstrousness and feel ridicule of my refinement, a demonstration that it is superfluous, in this vulgar hands-and-knees caricature. I despise him, his strength, his cunning, his self-evident mastery of this world. I despise the baboons one and all. The gluttons with the fat cheeks, they revolt me. Their unsightly public coupling and the self-abasing begging of the females, the ducking of the females under the hard hands of the males and the raucous scolding, and the eyes close together as you find them in brutes, and I think it is a sign of greed as well. I know too much about them for my taste. In a cage I would be able to laugh at them. As for what they know about me, they reveal nothing in those sidelong glances. I suppose I am no more than a nuisance to them. An outsider, far outside their realm of activity.

Only when I am asleep do I know fully who I am, for I reign over my dreamtime and occupy my dreams contentedly. At such times I am necessary to myself.

It was in a hurried flight from the sentry of a troop of sickle tails that I came upon a flattened patch – it looked flattened to me – and stumbled and sprawled and gasped for breath. I turned around. My heart beat down to my fingertips. The puffs of breath from my nostrils blew against quivering blades of dry grass.

Thus I lay for a long while with the resignation of a food scavenger to whom hunger is something familiar that can wait to be stilled. Then I saw something shining, little beads of light between my eyelashes shone green and black, the light turned to solid beads when with the tip of my finger I burrowed between the grass blades and touched them. Then I sat up and scratched the beads out of the dust and the dry roots. They lay on my palm, two black and one green. I carried the useless discovery to the tree.

They were as small as pollen. I examined them. I arranged them in the limited number of patterns that their number and colors allowed. I recognized them. The next day I wanted to return to the place where I found them, but the direction escaped me and aimlessly I searched, hoping that I would recognize a tree or a rock slope, for it was near a koppie, that I remembered, and I remembered the white stepladder of roots that a mountain fig had woven up against a rockface; but I found nothing. I roamed about in the veld as if I had not yet forced any system upon it, just like at the beginning when I arrived here.

Right at the beginning was no time, for there was no time to devote to sequence and there were no categories, since the scrabble to survive wiped these differences out. Now I can permit myself the luxury of classification, as well as a judicious application of old and newly acquired knowledge. I can even reflect on what I am doing. I can let my thoughts run consecutively and regularly, without waves or ripples, I can form my thinking round as a clay pot and set it down cool and precise as water, I can make the mouth of the clay pot stand out like a spout against the uncertainty of blue and of black air that penetrates me and fills me completely if I am not careful. And I fill my thoughts with all sorts of objects, endless row upon row, not to be counted, I thank providence, I can think of enough objects to obliterate everything, and in addition I can make up objects if the remembered ones run out. I have good remedies against being empty.

Here now, the little beads that do not require imagining and of a kind that I used to see hanging around the necks and wrists of men and women. Once they used to be accepted in exchange for things, just as I was accepted in exchange for something. Of course I have no idea what my value must have been or what it ever was. A piece of ring money. Countless pieces. Another area of which I have little knowledge is the expenditure of money. It was the privilege of a slave girl to have everything given to her. The roof over my head. The cloth around my body. The food – in my case, plenty of it. How happy I was.

The beads are so tiny that they are barely visible on the knot in the tree where I keep them; but with my eyes shut I would be able to pick them up. I know the interior of my tree as a blind man knows his home, I know its flat surfaces and grooves and swellings and edges, its smell, its darknesses, its great crack of light as I never knew the huts and rooms where I was ordered to sleep, as I can only know something that is mine and mine only, my dwelling place into which no one ever penetrates. I can say: this is mine. I can say: this is I. These are my footprints. These are the ashes of my fireplace. These are my grinding stones. These are my beads. My sherds.

A supreme being I am in my grey tree skin. When I appear in the opening I stand proudly. Afterwards I suspect that I pose in the easily cultivated attitude of apparently relaxed expectation that I learned to adopt before my owners, mindful of the advantage of making an impression and at the same time beneath the surface brimming with conceit because I held this tiny scrap of power.

But imperiously I stand now and gaze out over the veld, and every time I step outside the world belongs to me. Every time I step out from the protecting interior of the tree I am once again a human being and powerful, and I gaze far over the landscape with all its flourishes of vegetal growth and troops of animals and the purple patches of hills that try to hedge it in on the horizon. Reborn every time from the belly of the baobab, I stand full of myself. The sun defines my shadow. The wind clothes me. I point to the air and say: air make me live. And when the scrub warbler calls, he calls in my name. I am all there is, he calls.

Not everything is I. No. If there are still people here. Not everything.

How trifling the beads I have discovered compared with those I wore earlier, great oval red and yellow glass beads that hung like ripe berries around neck and wrists, complementing the ivory of a bracelet around my upper arm and my silk gown printed in shades of yellow. I was radiant. I laughed whitely. I was an object to be shown off, gloriously young as I first was. My marklessness, my smoothness, my onetime wholeness of skin. I was the envied uncircumcised one. I was the desired. I was too young to care in the slightest, to say nothing of understanding. I was a child. Such a child, such a child. I was still a child when I carried a child inside me.

Thankfully I remember the women who with their soothing gestures broke me in. Only here and there did I catch a reference, an intonation or an emphasis, for they spoke a language that poured down around me like a waterfall, it fell and fell from their mouths. Who were these women who adopted me and mothered me and taught me the game with men? I was overloaded with gifts to make me attractive. At the time I thought them gifts. I clamped myself fast to the women and tried to be good. Sometimes they scolded me. Then their lips opened and there was a creaking and crackling. But my tears were kissed away, they gave a clatter of friendly laughter, picked me up on their laps, pressed me to them, and I loved them like a child who once again feels safe; I climbed from lap to lap and jingled their bracelets. Thus, playing with me, they taught me, so that eventually I would remember the rapture and the torment, but inwardly remain untouched, remain whole, remain myself. I call you up in my memory. I cannot remember your faces but that does not matter. I remember your wonderful affection. I wonder whether you are now old and sad, and whether you still live in that house that was your destination, and whether you remember me, one of the multitude entrusted to your special soft playful care, and whether you ever tried to find out what happened to all of us. Whether you minded.

I never forgot your lessons, and even now I could laugh lewdly if I had to, and even now I could, like a cat, snuggle up lithely or wriggle free, and temper or increase my intensity as the situation demanded; but that has all become superfluous.

Now I live in a hollow with sleep the dense solution. I live in time measured by myself, initially with three beads, later with more and more till I chose the best of the green ones for my arrangement. So, to begin with, there passed in cycle a green day and two black days, later just a string of green days. Later I grew tired of green days and varied them with black in any conceivable pattern and number, as determined by mood and chance. My days became grouped. It was already a method to counter the vagueness of time hiding behind the course of nature. Time threatened me. It wanted to annihilate me. I thought I cheated it by changing my system every so often. Never did time know what I was going to try next, where even in the morning when light and chirruping awoke me I did not know what I was going to try with time, where I looked for firewood as and when necessary, fetched water when my supply was up, searched for food when I had to, and ate when I felt hungry, slept when drowsiness made my limbs heavy. And I dreamed and nodded through rose quartz.

I was reaching a stage of forgetting my counting toys, which then numbered only three and were gradually beginning to bore me, on the knot on the inner wall of the tree, when one day I picked up in various places more potsherds and beads as well as copper wire, and brought all this back. I added the rest, sherd and bead, to the heap, these leavings of inhabitants whom I wished ill because they could leave no more than this, potsherds that would not fit together and become a whole roundness, pitiful decorations that I irritably strung on stalks and carried around my neck, rusty copper-wire rings, thick and heavy as shackles, with which I could do nothing, and nothing more in my vicinity. Nothing more – or was I roaming over graves? Nothing more – or was I roaming over walls submerged in dust and overgrown with plants? Was I perhaps roaming over courtyards and squares, fortifications, terraces, conduits, halls and shanties, settlements and streets crumbled into insignificance, taken over by the winters and the summers? Was I roaming over the place that we aimlessly came looking for, purposefulness long ago relinquished in the pitiless sun? Place of strips of underbrush and prickly grass, of a river off to one side hidden behind ripine trees and creepers, of hills with flattened crests on which gigantic round rocks piled in fantastic shapes, place of my towering baobab? Tableaus through which we roamed dazed, frightened? Place of predator and prey?

I imagine bloody wars of extermination. Droughts. An epidemic. I think of unflagging zeal, followed by collapse and despair. And then nothing, just a tiny residue that does not help me however much I make believe I have found a way of warding off the danger of timelessness through order. Because I resisted becoming a mere yawn in the lazy passage of the days, a mere transitory draught of air, a subordinate beat in the rhythm, a phantom within a rupture in eternity.

Too scantily endowed to fashion something myself, I used the artefacts of forgotten people to while away time, to coagulate time, with the bitter realization that it was changing nothing in the nothingness.

But it made me feel good to handle the things and to wonder and to give my imagination rein, supplemented by memories of a different kind of earlier time.

For it was endowed with nothing but memories that I landed here, a famished, tattered being, struggling through plains and valleys, fevered with privation, stumbling on towards a steadily receding horizon, always day stages away, always the same, to be swallowed in by a tree, merciful harborage, merciful cool shelter that reminds one roughly of a building with walls and spout-shaped rising ceiling and earth for a floor, a giant hut crowned with branches and leaves.

Curse the will-o'-the-wisp that led me here, that traveler through my life and the lives of others on whose lips I hung and whom I slavishly obeyed, blind with obsession, disordered, out of my senses. Curse him who made a spectacle of our sacrifice and wanted to give the attractiveness of understanding to hardship, the attractive useless self-knowledge that killed him, oh the talk, the talk, the omniscience, the all-investigating consciousness that could explain nothing, least of all the betrayal of comrade and following. Oh, the powerlessness of reasonableness!

Stranger in msasa-red clothes, from the beginning his wit charmed me. He knew the quips that light up an all too gloomy conversation. He knew more points of the compass than the disputatious poets and other such celebrities who congregated in the home of my owner, the rich widowed merchant, to eat my well-prepared meals and to pay for them and for the intercourse with his pretty slave girls with sophisticated conversation, even if this was limited to looking and desiring, or at most to some daredevil trying to fondle them when he thought his host was looking the other way. This one, on the other hand, in his msasa-red, in his water-green, in his flame-yellow, this one with his gold-speckled necklaces and slim gold bracelets was in no small measure well-read and self-confidently informed about affairs. Without being asked he delivered a rejoinder, briefly summed up long-windedness, and time and again carried the arguments to ridiculous ends. Which made him little loved among our great spirits, who without success egged him on and tried to catch him in sacrilege or sedition. Let the gods stare over our heads. They know what they see. He asserted. Let the ancestors alone. Their intercession is not needed when you live unimpeachably.

Isn't that so? he asked. Isn't that so?

As fresh and new as lightning he put it to me.

So too the intercession of the prophets and the intercession of the family members of the prophets and the intercession of the gods combined and the intercession of god-fearing people, as well as the moral lessons to be learned from the experiences of people who elevate their tribal history to a religion – all this is interesting, and long may it be so. And invoking a deity morning and evening is beautiful music, is a resonant component of the sounds with which a man attests that he not only thinks of food and propagation but considers himself immortal as well and therefore wants to take appropriate measures to ensure himself a pleasant afterlife. Let them. Let them by all means.

And let the merchants carry on. They are providing all this prosperity – and with an eloquent gesture he handed a porcelain dish of shrimps stewed with rice in sesame oil and coconut milk to the peevish poet on his right, while smiling in my direction. I thought he winked at me.

My owner's sardonic gaze rested on me. He beckoned me closer and his copper bracelets fell from his wrist to his elbow, so thin had his arm become. I picked up the palm fan to fan him. His upper lip was damp with droplets of sweat. Tonight he would again shiver with fever. He was already a sick man, probably dying, when I moved in with him and dared to become his youngest favorite. With long regular movements I tried to stir the heavy air around his face. He had left his food untouched, just tasted a dish of water. Poor creature inexorably gasping out a rich man's life with the spectacle of so much abundance before him. Influence and power slipped out of mouth and nostrils. Stored-up memories played themselves out in his cloudy eyes when the eyelids, between the spells when he sat and dozed, opened a slit and he presumably observed his guests, his slave girl servants, his sons and daughters gathered in luxury and pride. And his emaciated fingers, what were they trying to catch? A butterfly? The salt breeze? A woman's laugh?

The talk grew dull. He asked to be carried to his room. I say asked, not commanded. He asked in a whisper.

Left alone with him, I held him tight and soothed him, for he rebelled against his weakening and was far too fidgety; but then out of pity I let him be and by watching I understood what his hand was grasping for. He was trying to tear the fine web that death was spinning around him. When he jerked in spasms the web vibrated and shimmered slyly in anticipation. Tighter and tighter it was spun around him, so that the threat of sounds outside the room could not penetrate and the murmur of people with concern or concerns remained far outside the ring of his death stillness.

I let the invalid nestle between my drawn-up knees with his head on my breast. In his language I whispered lewd stories which made him smile blissfully in my arms. Shrunken baby, what an easy delivery for me. I fed you with the deathsmilk of indifference, for it could do your dried-out body no more harm and perhaps it was your way out, this being set free of any charitableness. Any pity would only delay your departure painfully.

One morning I climbed up to the highest terrace on the roof of my owner's house to breathe in the morning freshness and look out over the city and the sea, at the skiffs lying drawn up on the sand, several of them belonging to him whom I had just said farewell to forever, that would probably now, like me, be disposed of. My future and the future of my fellow slaves, women and men, as well as that of the skiffs over there in the rosy daybreak, as well as that of the stores of elephant tusks and ambergris and iron, and that of the great house now at last plunged into mourning, and that of his fragrant garden down below me, had been allotted a precarious fate. Only those who have, have security as well. For me there was only insecurity. I waited, expecting to sigh. I waited for my feelings to well up. It was now the time for that.

I who come from the heart of the country bear the murmur of waters subliminally with me, a water knowledge preserved in my

tears and saliva, in the blood of my veins, in all the juices of my body.
I who knew how to extinguish attacks of fever with my water being,
I found myself crying uncontrollably here in the morning stillness
about so many things all at once that I would try to sob my tangle
of thoughts to death rather than seek an interpretation that would
amount to mourning but also a feeling of relief, anxiety about the
future but also plain happiness about the purity of the morning after
the oppressiveness of days and days in a sickroom.

With a corner of my robe I dried my eyes and cheeks and climbed
back down to the garden. I had to find out what was going on. I
walked down to the beach and from there – for my call to the solitary
dhow in the bay remained unanswered – from there I walked through
the neglected waterfront area, hoping that no one would notice my
absence in the bustle and diminished supervision that follow such an
important death. And even if they did notice it, what did I care. I was
dumbfounded with grief, but more, with longing, and did not care
who saw it. My longing was a hard little nut hidden deep within me. I
did not care who knew of it now. Now, after my benefactor's decease,
this feeling was my only certainty, and it helped me forget my fear
of what lay ahead. Frivolous, perhaps, if I had been a woman who
could have decided her own fate, but surely a permissible escape for
the owned class to which I belonged. To fall foolishly in love and try
to pocket happiness where happiness waited visible through a chink,
and the time possibly favorable.

So now I searched for the man I had fallen in love with. I heard him
laugh behind a heavy, richly carved teak door in secret consultation

in his life away from me. I saw him disappear round a corner. I smelled him out, wherever he might stay, where he might yet walk, for he had promised to come again, and he would come again over the swell on the lee side of a billowing lateen sail, and I followed him in my imagination where the hem of his robe dragged through the mud, brushed over the fleshiness of a broken melon, and whisked over sand and fins and scales. I lingered with him where he stopped before the market women, occupied in observing how the poorest of the poor lived. Clouds of flies swarmed up from the piles of grilled fish and meat. They settled in patterns against the blue of this clothes and crawled over his nose and eyes and forehead, at the wet corners of his mouth, wherever there was moisture.

An old acquaintance came shuffling along with a flat basket of plantains on her head which she put down with a groan; then she took up position with legs stretched out in her traditional place under the shade tree. He began to chat to her and to others round about. He listened to brusque surly answers, embarrassed answers or equally embarrassed silences, to eagerly supplied information and quick-witted remarks in answer to questions from him, this presumptuous gentleman who was certainly not a client, making his own deductions. And with his inquiries about the price of crabs and clams and mussels and the availability and readiness to hand or otherwise of meat and fish and firewood, he built up cases using his own information, acquired on the spot, with which to refute other later arguments, opposing this information to the vague theories of rulers and well-meaning people. An attentive man. An inquisitive person who came to acquaint himself with the lot of the lowest, so much more complicated than the easy existence of a slave girl in a generous household, as he often pointed out to me.

My easy, indolent existence, yes, an existence now perhaps at an end.

Where did I find myself now, and was this smell of smoldering fear not familiar to me? The stench of blood. From this fear I never escaped, this trusty dizziness that impaired my sight, that made me brush with my hand over my eyes to see better and made me rue the act at once, for where I found myself, I discovered, was very near the slaughterhouse where I was sometimes sent by my second owner to buy entrails for his slaves. This smell known all too well to me, this lowing and bleating. Slippery heart liver lungs and gullet messily wrapped in leaves, a messiness too prone to slip out to carry on my head, I held it before me a little way from my body and walked away from a desolation soiled with dung and filth where animals buckled at the knee and the sad palms in their long dresses rustled dry leaves and grated, powerlessly anchored. Walked off from the joking butchers' teasing and provocative remarks and obscene gestures to go and cook the food that I would share with many mouths, and plot how to keep the liver aside for myself and mine, and how to pinch a scoopful of my master and his wife's rice in the – advantageously for me – untidy running of the household.

In two low huts with collapsed roofs we lived, the slaves, all together, not separated by sex. From sunrise to late at night we toiled for him, the spice merchant. The work was what separated us. The men worked in his warehouse on the waterfront and the women in his residence. From far and wide we came, we spoke a variety of tongues, but here we got along by mangling the natives' language and turning it into our idiosyncratic workers' language. We were acquired second-hand, third-hand, even fourth-hand, mostly still young and healthy, we women fertile and rank. At night it was legs apart for the owner on his sweaty skin rug. Some of us welcomed it. Not I. He was clumsy and rough. I envied the slaves exempted from this sort of service. It brought a certain freedom along with it, after all, to be unmanned, I thought. I did not mind standing in front of the fireplace. I did not mind toiling with pick and hoe in the garden in the murderous heat to keep it neat around his mango trees and yam vines. I did not mind tidying his house under the eye of his shrew of a wife, obeying her expressionlessly, keeping my murmurs for the sleeping quarters, and even there being careful, for there were tell-tales amongst us. And to be discovered meant that your tongue was cut out.

I kept myself to myself. Lived as much uneasily as patiently. I was a coward and refused nothing.

With a stiff face I listened on his skin rug to the noise of the sea. I became a shell plucked from the rocks but kept my oyster shell of will, my thin deposit of pride, kept myself as I had been taught. I did not give in. I did not surrender. I let it happen. I could wait. I listened to the beat of the waves far behind his groaning, and it lulled me. I was of water. I was a flowing into all kinds of forms. I could preserve his seed and bring it to fruition from the sap of my body. I could kneel in waves of contractions with my face near to the earth to which water is married, and push the fruit out of myself and give my dripping breasts to one suckling child after another. My eyes smiled. My mouth was still.

Always still. Frightened mice in the middle of a great roaring, that was what we were, the subordinates of the system, apparently docile, our children taken away from us and sold while still infants, while our bodies still hungered for them, our past a past of pitiless mistreatment or the sarcasm of gifts, our present without prospect. We were all one woman, interchangeable, exchangeable. So we comforted each other and each other's children, so we shared, so we looked for lice on each other's scalps and wore each other's clothes and sang together, gossiped together, complained together. Without prospect. Once someone tried to run away. She was caught and her feet chopped off. A second time someone tried. She got away. The eunuchs deserted regularly.

There were stories current about a colony of deserters far from the city in the middle of the great swamp, where the escaped slaves lived by hunting, where they built mat huts and survived unbearable heat and loneliness to die there eventually as free people. It was said that they had developed their own system of government, with a headman and advisers, that they considered themselves safe, protected from the pursuit by the impenetrable swamp infested with mosquitoes and leeches whose secret paths only the initiated knew, that they knew the authorities winked at them seeing that it would have cost a great deal of money to bring them back, seeing that those who had escaped would always be looking for trouble, would always grumble and rebel, and that it was wiser to punish such rebellious souls with oblivion in the wilderness, seeing that there were anyhow always fresh consignments of slaves coming from the interior. And that the eunuchs did not allow slave women among them.

One day a storm blew up worse than any I had yet experienced. It felt as if the heat were taking possession of me. It felt as if my eyes were going to bulge and stand out on stalks like a crab's. I pressed my palms hard against my eye sockets, for it felt as if sand and glass splinters were rasping over my unprotected stalk eyes, as if they beheld too much and too tenderly, therefore I tried to press them into my skull, but they throbbed so violently in my head, they rolled around inside my skull, and when my eyelids opened, I saw nothing, I saw only heat, and that made everything roll and heave. I could no longer hear anything. I could only feel in the pitch-black air that came towards me and drew away from me and began to push me around, to tug me in gusts this way and that way, to bring me face to face with rending lightning bolts that transformed everything into gaudiness and in a flash blacked everything out again and left me totally confused as to the direction I had been taking. I saw a bitter-orange tree where none had stood before. I saw a grey cloud consisting of crested terns and a second cloud thick with glistening sardines. I saw fishes rain and jellyfish tumble down and flotsam performing tricks and saw how a hut sucked in air till bursting point and suddenly collapsed and was flattened and suddenly began to whirl away in pieces.

Then I fled before the wind that was snatching up me and the refuse and everything that was frail, and I struggled onward at a slant, half-crawling, reeling from one support to the next, tree, pole, gate, building. That I could be blown into space, I, the peels, the tatters, go up in the whirl into all eternity. The sea beating. It fought with itself. It drew apart and clashed and balled together, it drew itself up high into the sky, it beat thunderously down on the high-water mark and rolled over and over covering the city's shanty quarter and the luxuriant woods there, and hurled pieces of wreckage from dhows and skiffs that had been made for and dedicated to it, down between the palms and rosebushes of the gardens of the rich. The wind tore the sails loose from the trees where they tried to hide like the ghosts of birds and blew them far away into the strange interior.

The sea drew back hissing over its destruction, drew in a last tortured, foaming breath, and subsided to a gloomy calm, and the wind subsided too, leaving such a rarefied stillness that a sob could have shattered it.

This brittle peace lasted only briefly. There was a patter of drops. At once it became pouring rain. Dense sheets came racing on over a sea that had totally forgotten its brief calm and heaved swollen and confused as the tide dragged it one way and the wind pushed it another. Pouring rain, gouts of water, hard and vertical, drops that mutilated the surface of the street into pockmarks, water that streamed and scoured out and washed away what the wind had forgotten to blow away and ran off in clattering furrows. A thorough, purposeful, seething rain. A storm rain with a mission.

Someone must have heard me moaning. Someone must have heard me whimpering where I lay trapped under a branch of a kudu-berry tree, a tree that, under orders from the storm, wanted to claim me as sacrifice because I had always resolutely ignored it and never tried to seek the favor of its spirit, because I ignore all spirits save that which lives in me. Probably because I did not know better. Perhaps. Perhaps I was obstinately defiant where I had brought nothing of my own with me and local rituals appeared without content, and I created my own rituals for my own indwelling spirit and without preknowledge went and picked up a white shell and a black shell. Placate the spirit of the earth, the spirit of the house, of the air, bring an offering of atonement, recite rhymes, mumble a formula, placate the spirit of the tree, he listens, he notes your gesture of sacrifice, he will watch over you, only be careful when you talk – no, that meant nothing to me. I smiled at the gestures. I walked nonchalantly past all the kudu-berry trees, which had after all been planted here and there on street corners only for their fierce autumn colors and had not come to grow here for my sake. I walked past them head in the air and offered them nothing. No, I laughed at the other women who bowed before them and reverently set down a handful of millet grains on the great leaf of a fever tree beside the silent tree trunk and muttered over them. I did not mutter at all, not for any tree spirit in the world. My tongue is meant for me, my tongue, my mouth, my whole self is mine. I pressed my ear against the grey-brown trunk of the kudu-berry and listened attentively to hear if its spirit had anything to say, but I heard only wood slowly groaning, slowly expanding the chronicle of its year rings, and I knew he would not have anything to say one day about a woman who once pressed her head against him, just as little as he would have stories to tell about other simpletons who begged his blessings. This was my considered opinion long, long before I myself was looked upon as the spirit of a tree.

And then the kudu-berry punished you, my benefactor joked, he who sent his slaves to free me from the branch after he had been notified of the accident right in front of his house. He gave me shelter in his slave quarters till the broken bone I had suffered healed. But even then before I was literally back on my feet he became my third owner.

So he must have found delight in me. So I must have afforded him pleasure. One evening he came to inquire about the condition of the chance patient in his care, and looked surprised when I laughed at the superstition about the kudu-berry tree, and drew me out on my short history, as self-contained and boring as the history of most of the slave girls in the city. In a brief and concise transaction he bought me, and my stay began in all humility in the high residence with the terrace roof built of stone from a far-off quarry, with a view over the low-lying city and the sea, with neat outbuildings and well-tended inner courtyards. My benefactor often summoned me. We spoke. The night came when he slept with me. He found me charming. More often than he had sexual intercourse with me, he ordered me to undress and simply talk to him quietly, while he kept looking at me as one views a pretty sunset or something like that. In the same way he looked at his son's serval cat. When his bouts of fever came over him, only I was allowed to stay with him, and I sat and fanned him.

Fellow slaves of my second owner, who had stayed behind in misery – I had no chance to grieve for you. It had happened that the hurricane elected me. I was in agreement with what was befalling me.

I hankered for nothing, I moped about nothing, I could not get excited about anything in my past, and in fact was unwilling to talk about it. It was wasted time. For I was becoming possessed with myself.

Now for the first time I discovered beauty, my own and that of bunches of flowers, and of soapstone statuettes and jade clasps and porcelain glaze, and of batiks dyed with indigo, and of lovely silk, light as a breath or heavy and stiff and interwoven with gold. It was almost as if I were learning again to talk. I occupied myself in refined tasks like complicated embroidery, which was taught to me by older slave women, and the preparation of dishes for a banquet for a roomful of visitors, and the tasteful serving thereof. In the last-named I excelled. I learned to converse quite differently, with a metallic tone of irony at the tail end of a remark. I learned to make my voice dove-sweet when the conversation became pointed and too many quick remarks, like slim arrowheads, were being shot off all together. I learned to laugh with abandon.

Above all I learned to find pleasure in how to look desirable and in the power it was obviously supposed I could exercise to my own advantage in my benefactor owner's room. He gave me an ivory bracelet which fitted around my left upper arm and which I shamelessly showed off. Often I referred cattishly, when he was in the right mood, to the other slave girls' most glaring defects: to thin calves, knobbly shoulders, missing teeth, breasts out of proportion, jutting chins, fingers as rough as a chimpanzee's; and though he playfully agreed, and although he claimed that such shortcomings were limited and made little difference on the couch of pleasure, as he jokingly called his sleeping mat, I knew that what I had said remained in his thoughts. But I got only one bracelet from him.

Nevertheless. Nevertheless. My life shone. I hummed as I rubbed my skin with coconut oil. Only later did I find out that he had two kinds of slaves in service, one kind for their looks, the other kind for their readiness to serve.

So what was the source of melancholy that sometimes attacked me? As I looked out from the terrace over the sparkling bay and saw the dhows and skiffs wink there, as I looked over the roofs towards the haziness of the horizon and grew dulled with a stupid restlessness here within me and the screech of a gull frightened me, what were my hands doing in front of my face? What could I have to feel sorrowful about? Now that the fondness of my newest owner, wealthy widower and foremost citizen, like cool moss coolly and softly protected me and I felt cozily hidden in his care, not just feeling safe but surmising the sparkle of a new time of life for me here in the looser relationship in which I now lived and in which my talents dared to unfold and there was little to restrict me – why did the tears well up in my eyes and the city tremble in refracted colors? Why did my head sink on my chest? Why did I try to make myself as insignificant as possible, look for a dark corner, pretend absence when I was called?

I sat, tiny as a beetle, and whined. I was so full of held-in whining that I was ready to burst. I wished that I had a snout with which to burrow into the earth and disappear, or into the bark of a tree where I could lurk inconspicuously, pressed flat.

This was the mood I knew best. I knew it from long back. I have known it here, too, I admit honestly to you, trusty baobab, confidant, home, fort, water source, medicine chest, honey holder, my refuge, my last resort before a change of residence over which I shall have no control at all, my midpoint, guardian of my passionate outbursts, leafless coagulated obesity winter and summer life-giving rocking cupola of leaves and flowers and sour seeds that I press to my cheek (the grey-green fur strokes my skin), that I break open to roast your kernels and devour them, hanging like fulfillment from you, directed to the earth, waiting. You protect me. I revere you. That is to say, the fieldmouse and I inhabit you, but only I revere you, I think, only I.

If I could write, I would take up a porcupine quill and scratch your enormous belly full from top to bottom. I would clamber up as far as your branches and carve notches in your armpits to make you laugh. Big letters. Small letters. In a script full of lobes and curls, in circumambient lines I write round and round you, for I have so much to tell of a trip to a new horizon that became an expedition to a tree. Here comes a rhythmic pause. Oh, I have learned much from the poets, I am versed in the techniques, in the patching together of lyric and epic. Rhythmic pause and on roll the thoughts, round and round your trunk the poetic history of a crazy eagerness that was finally all we could cling to, stripped of material things and emaciated and tired to death of ourselves in the endeavor that transported us along, ballast of the past.

Thus I decorate you line after line with our hallucinations so that you can digest, outgrow, make smooth this ridiculousness, preserve the useless information in your thick skin till the day of your spontaneous combustion. And satisfied I put down the porcupine quill and stand back to regard my handiwork, hands on my hips. You are full of my scars, baobab. I did not know I had so many.

If I could write. Even then, melancholy would take possession of me. Wearily I take the path to the river, there in the cool to fill my being with the sounds of my sister-being, to refresh myself in the modest scents of pigeonwood and mitzeerie, to let my gaze end in a tangle of monkey ropes and fern arches and the slowly descending leaves, and to find rest, all day long, all night long.

There is always an ape to defile a sanctuary. How irritated I get when animals do not stay within the limits of their animal nature but want to address me on my level. For instance, the troop of samangos in the top of the water-berry tree. As if they were being sold short by me, as if I represented a great threat, as if I did not also belong, but had to be driven off with reproaches and deep warnings. Glare at me impudently indeed. Reprimand me indeed. Confront me and show disapproval indeed.

So too the grey parrot that my benefactor kept. Cool disapproval, ridicule, derision in the little eyes. If he wished you good morning he meant to push off, and the eyes became small as dots. He turned language inside out so that the meaning fell out and nothing could be said. He fouled his cage. He woke the whole household with his noise and challenged you when you hushed him with such a clear whistle that it split the air with its purity; and he, the prisoner, triumphed. That he with his puny bird intellect could learn how to triumph while I was plagued with depression, and acted uncertainly, and showed that

I felt hurt, and defended myself with acrimony, said sneering things behind their backs about the two sons and one daughter who still lived in the house, made myself unloved among the slaves.

Wholly different my relation with the tame serval of the house. How often did I not wish I could scrape together the courage to blandly slip the catch on the door of the parrot's cage so that he could fly out, the idiot, so that the serval should suddenly jump up from behind a bush somewhere and slap him unconscious in the air and grab him. Then he would carry him off in his mouth and grindingly eat him up, grindingly, till there was nothing left but one grey feather and one red. End of parrot.

Down below in the courtyard walked the speckled cat. He scraped his cheek against a plane bush and a scattering of scarlet, jasper-green and black blossoms sifted down on to him and grey-white tatters of bark stuck to his snout. He snorted in surprise. Then he trotted off, taking a shortcut across the paving, with decidedly and certainly a most important objective in mind. He paid no attention to my call. He had pinned a gecko with his forepaw, I saw, and was considering what to do next; first he looked up at me, then with cat-specific dissimulation at his prey. I stared at him. I could stare for long into his changeable eyes and imagine we were one of spirit. He yawned hugely with tongue curled back and as he yawned looked terrifyingly cruel. Yet this illusion was enough to make me understand that we were not playmates and that there was a distance to be maintained between us, which I would keep, I promised him, and stroked his fur and scratched behind his ears. Black-snout-sweet-face, your self-sufficiency amused me. Perhaps we had more in common than you would think.

As a kitten he was made a present to my owner's youngest son, who as a young boy had apparently collected wild animals as a hobby. In the time of which I speak the son's interest was concentrated mainly on fishing and one barely saw him at home, for from early till late he was aboard his extremely expensive proa. But when he was here I enjoyed his wonderfully healthy roughness and his boyishness, and enjoyed all his pranks. Young frolicsome man, most attractive, and so serious and laughably touchy when it came to his hobby. I consciously call it his hobby because I did not believe his father would allow him to choose fishing as a career, unless perhaps, unless it could be administered as a subdivision of the family's business and the boy could then, as befitted a scion of the wealthy, do business and not haul in the nets like a poor simple fisherman.

Now I knew why I felt depressed. I had seen the procession. Well, I knew they were to be expected. Knew they had to turn up some time or other, and therefore went up to the root every blessed day to keep watch, to keep an eye out to see what I had promised myself I would not look at. The terrible procession, nerve-rackingly slow. I saw them coming from afar from my look-out post and beheld, fascinated despite myself, the signs of brokenness that rent me, crushed my spirit, made me stare despairingly, made me note their fate helplessly every time and keep my sympathies in check, force myself to joke about them so that I could forget and repress. My eyes followed them from where they appeared out of the bushes and bulrushes at the seam of the unraveling residential quarters and wove through the harsh planes of shadow and sunlight on the streets, sometimes disappearing from my field of vision, but I knew the route too well and settled my unwilling gaze in advance on the point where they must reappear; at the head of a few of the men in service, armed but on foot like their human prey, followed by a primitive sedan chair on which the slave hunter sat at rest, rocking on the shoulders of two of his captives, the big boss no longer half-asleep as on the immeasurably long bush path that they had all covered, but wide-awake now that the moment, the most important moment was about to dawn, followed by those in chains, some with packs of leopard skins, elephant tusks, rhinoceros horns and provisions on their heads, their faces twisted as the neck irons chafed them, followed by the young women and tender little girls shackled to each other with lighter chains. So they trod reluctantly on to the place of destination. At the tail a rearguard of more armed men.

I followed them. I knew where. I took a shortcut through side streets and alleys and across open unbuilt spaces and arrived at the square near the beach before them, and hid behind the tattered dusty castor-oil trees there and the scanty undergrowth around. The arrival of a fresh consignment of slaves was proceeding normally and attracted no one's attention. Only I was all unwilling eyes.

Clinking, my fellows in fate arrived. The untouched girls, my little sisters. The young eunuchs, no longer men, no longer human beings, the survivors of a raid deep into the interior, my own people half-people may not be people, the compelled, the pitifully strong healthy products. They stood still. They were allowed to sit.

The sedan chair was set down. The slave hunter stood up stiffly and stretched, a pleasant long stretch, before he got off his chair and turned his steps towards the city to discuss business over a bowl of fig wine and a pipe of hashish. He was an old man, I saw. He had grey patches of beard at the point of his chin, but he strode quickly as if refreshed by the sea air and cheered up by a sense of relief that the difficult undertaking had gone off successfully as far as the coast. The guards stayed at their post. I wondered if they had been here before. I wondered if the complement of the slaves was full and how many had grown so weak from exhaustion along the road that they had been left behind as unserviceable, and how many of them had perished of marsh fever, and how many had grown rebellious and been killed. Those who were left now lay in silence on the ground. Even some of the guards had sat down.

On the beach a group of urchins were kicking sand at a dead hammerhead shark. They rushed about and barked and growled, pretending to be dogs, and laughed and jumped with exuberance over the shark. They laughed their joy out. They lost interest in the leathery carcass and careered further up the beach looking for fun, picked switches and chased each other further along the foamline of the waves, splashing in the shallows. Brief happiness disappeared from the air. The sultry stillness again closed in.

A few days ago I had seen the hammerhead shark leaping in spasms there on the beach where fish-drying racks cast their grid shadows.

It was trying to lift its whole body up from the sand as if wanting to swim upwards into the sky. Sometimes one eye was buried in the sand, sometimes the other; one saw doom, the other spied hope, and in uncertainty the poor thing struggled. Spasmodic jerks, fanatical till death, eyes that till death bisected the world. Would he, even in death, have to reconcile one half with the other half to find his way in that haze? Deeper and deeper he steered himself on into death with twisting movements of the head. To the left hung death as a grey apparition, to the right hung death as a grey apparition, no choice for him, but perhaps he fabricated his own death and chose the total nothing of seeing nothing more, and nothing has neither tinge nor grain nor substance.

I was not permitted to offer refreshments to the new arrivals. I had already tried that in the past and been chased away. Nevertheless I went closer. In my worker's language I softly welcomed them and expressed my commiseration; but it seemed that no one heard or understood me. Nevertheless I talked to them because I knew of nothing else, and most of all of nothing more effective, to do.

I told them all I knew about my origins. Humbly I offered them the scanty history. My facts I patched together as they occurred to me, my memory of a journey with fear the starting point and fear the end point. I was well grounded in the knowledge of fear. I had felt him in my blood vessels, for he had come to live in me and I had begun to smell like him, and with his eyes I had seen forests and plains shift by poisonous and distorted; with his ears I had listened, and there was a growling, and even the stillness rumbled, and there was bitterness in my cheeks. Oh, fear is by no means whatsoever a connoisseur of events. He gobbles up everything. He crushes everything. He leaves no bloody trail behind because he stands still. Everything comes to him, feels drawn to him, and he knows it.

I don't know. This I know: that I allayed fear and terror in and through my dreams and that thereby I rendered harmless the nameless, the formless. But I had to learn to do that. It was the outcome of affliction. It is something I still do.

This I know: that I was not condemned as these people were, because on the day of my arrival, so I was told, I, the only girl captured, exempted from chains, wandered away from the others, shot down to the sea and picked up a white shell and a black shell. For I am of water. I know what turns the air to water. Then, so they say, it began to rain. Rain, rain drizzled down.

I turned my back on the damned. I was the head slave girl of the richest man here. I had more power than many a wife. Love of ease characterized my life. A lazy contemplation of the stupidity of others, that I could afford, with the symbol of my owner's pleasure in me around my arm like a reprimand to those who would like to humiliate me. Even if the bouts of depression came too often, too often, I gritted my teeth: it dared not get the upper hand. My existence was pomp and circumstance, was sparkle and excitement, was shining rippling water over a bed of pebbles, was secret well water's blessing upon the lips, was sea water's beneficence and power.

Like a baby laid on its stomach, curling its spine as it tries to curl upright, so the hammerhead shark had struggled.

Hurriedly, seeing blind, I went over to the dead one and buried him in the sand with my hands, and on my knees sat before the little grave and cried and did not stop. It brought me no relief. I did not stop.

I cannot remember that, since coming to live in the baobab, I have ever cried so bitterly. From rage, yes, often. From frustration, at the beginning, when I was still struggling to light a fire, the knack of the friction-stick escaping me and the spark simply not leaping. Or when, unequipped stupid civilized creature, I tried to search out tubers in the tracks of baboon and warthog, food intended only exceptionally for the human system, as I was to discover with sorrow when stomach cramps made me writhe in pain. I ate locusts – the hoppers. Exulted when I chanced on a jackal food flower that porcupine and baboon had missed. I disdained my nose's warning and in a sweat dug the fruit out, only to bring up before I could put my mouth to the gruesome brown musky bluebottle lure. I get sick when I think of it. I get glassily sick. I pulled grass stalks out of their protective leaves and chewed the juicy white lower points. I tried to steal birds' eggs, but was too clumsy a climber. I did not even get to the nests. I did not have the sharpness of vision to discern ground nests in the grass veld.

In time I grew emaciated and dulled. My weakness affected my sight. Plants, trees, stumps, stones, antheaps changed before my cloudy gaze into billowing lines that resolved themselves in frighten-ingly beautiful arrangements and left me floating and penetrated my sleep, for now I slept most of the time, I slept on the heaving colors, they made for rest in their restlessness, I did not try to control them, they washed lovingly over me, rolled me considerately over, I bathed in them and sighed contentedly.

Then I got up, wide-awake, and wandered about like a fool in the paradisal luxuriance. This was a garden! Let me acquaint myself with it. To the eye uncared for and full of thorns, full of brambles. Let me inspect again. The berries hid mischievously. I had to learn the game better. A clusterleaf offered winged fruit. But was it for me? Was it a clusterleaf? Let me walk further in the waves of heat, in the visible unfamiliar abundance. Every tree was a tree full of whistling. It made me light-headed. The noise. The exuberance. The confidence. The crazy-colored buntings frisking about.

I discovered a creeper with orange-red fruit full of thick spines that had wound itself around a tree, and its fruit seemed to me so pretty, so enticing, but I was sure they would be poisonous, I was sure they were not for me. Let me rather pass by. Nevertheless, I turned back and approached and picked one. Perhaps I should just try. I dared not. It was a bitter-apple of death, be warned. The fruit hung so nicely. I broke off the point of a spine. The flesh was light green. I pressed my tongue carefully to it and registered a pleasant taste. I tasted more of it. Ate it up. And for days waited to be sick. Then ran joyfully to the tree where the divine creepers grew and picked all the fruit and ate it all up, even those the birds had pecked. To this fruit I wanted to give a name. But I could not think of anything suitable. I called it the red spine fruit of the twining plant that in the winter adorns the camel's foot tree against the rise over there. I was far too scared to take honey out of the nest in the top of my home so as to store away provisions for the winter. I devised plans, oh yes, I thought myself to distraction, but I remained frightened. To be hungry and to know of a source of food and not to be able to get it.

To be hungry like the beggars in the city were, and the other outcasts, like the lepers banned to the bush and those who got pox and were rejected, and the lame and the crippled, those who tried to get by with a wooden stump, the blind with turned-over eyes and a child to lead them and help ask for alms. I gave nothing. I possessed nothing and could give nothing. With distaste I looked away. They pursued me with the fury of the desperate and stretched out their hands to me and looked at me urgently; they were so obtrusive, so dirty and full of sores. I was not my owner, and particularly not his eldest son, who scattered handfuls of cross money in the mud, on which the beggars descended as greedily as gulls, fighting over it and kicking up a comical hubbub. An uproarious, squalid, frenzied struggle for life would then take place in the streets on the outskirts of the city. In which I had no part. It was as if they were ready to bite and tear one another, peck one another till blood came. Here I was simply an unwilling spectator. In my time of hardship earlier . . . Admittedly I was looked after. I regularly got a bite to eat, that is true. There was an airy palm-frond roof over my head that leaked miserably in the rainy season and was never repaired. I had cotton clothes, threadbare with age, to cover my nakedness. I could exist. Admittedly. Certainly. Despite. In dullness I nosed around and kept body and soul together by drudgery. In tedium went on. Admittedly, that too was life. One of the slave girls in service with my second owner became bosom friends with me, and we tried to help each other as far as we could. She preferred laundry, I cooking. We ignored the other slave girls and divided the work as it suited us, even though it made them berate us, we knew they would gain nothing by going to complain to the man who owned us. To him we were all identical labor units. The two of us had wonderful jokes about him. We discussed his ugly habits to the finest detail, for example fiddling with himself or getting up halfway through intercourse to go and make water outside. Perhaps he suffered from incontinence. My bosom friend and I went into paroxysms over him and his nose-in-the-air wife, the old dry one, the old barren one.

Our children were plump and thriving in poverty, and we made no distinction between hers and mine. She carried mine on her back, I hers. She suckled mine, I hers. I was midwife to her, she to me. A child was a child to us. A warm little body in our arms, a dribbling little mouth searching for the nipple, the one's fat little neck as pretty as the other's, the one's teething as annoying as the other's. We brought them shells to play with, plaited a reed rope for them to skip with. Such a warm community, we and the infants. When it was my turn to cook I pinched some of the coconut milk and smuggled it back to them; and she in turn took them along to the washing stones at the river where they could make a mess undisturbed. Such a satisfying, lovely fullness that made up for so much in our shabby lives.

She was some years older than me. Had been through the same as me.

She and I had been through the following:

Caught young, not yet circumcised, for just that reason sought and caught. Among screaming women and old men, among the corpses of able-bodied men who had fought to the death or could not flee in time, among the burning huts, the beaten-down kraal fence, the destroyed millet containers, in the thick grass that offered no hiding place, in vain pulled behind a broad trunk by someone who wanted to save you, it was in vain. It was a vain scream of fear. It was a small commotion in a wide forest. It drew no more attention than the noise of a troop of apes. After the interruption the birds went on twittering. The hesitant bongo stepped into the open patch, cautiously smelled the odor of ash and decay and violence and the sweat of fear, and made an about turn, noiselessly. It rained. Slime and mud remained, black pools of putrefaction, of a sunken history. How hugely sighed the storms. How ceremoniously rocked the trees. Rose the sun. Turned the stars.

My friend told: How she first saw the sea, and she was afraid of the blue wall, the bank that rolled over and crashed.

I told: Here too I first saw the sea, but I was not afraid at all. I ran towards it.

My friend told: The man with whom she then went to live was very friendly. He was like a father.

I told: It was the same one. He bought the very youngest at the market. He cracked them as one cracks young pods. He was considerate and permitted you to have your firstborn under his roof, then he sold you.

He bought the very youngest. He broke the soft membrane like a blister. You were the spread-out one from whom blood flowed. You caught your breath, from pain and from what was surely ecstasy.

I told: He promised me a present. He gently pulled me closer, where he sat, till I was standing between his legs. He undressed me himself and let his hands roam lightly over my body. Then he licked me. Then he pointed to his headrest with the pretty snake bean and mother-of-pearl intarsia and promised me just such a one if I was good. Yes, I would be good. The women in his household had taught me what to do and what to answer; I nodded. He was out of breath and in a hurry.

I got my present; what about yours? I asked my friend.

Yes, she said.

Where are our headrests now? we laughed.

Mine was too big for me. My neck was still too short.

Mine too, I said.

Do you miss it?

No.

Does he still buy the very youngest ones?

He is dead.

No! When?

Long ago – long ago. His heart stopped.

What a pity! He is dead. He was actually quite kind-hearted.

Yes.

Yes, he was. Really. Funny and kind-hearted. And we could really stay with him till after the first confinement.

Oh, I was the sweetest little mother, I remember. Played at swelling for nine months, assiduously helped to make preparations, clumsy but very willing. I sucked a tamarind stone and spat it out. A mother-child, that's what I was. From my young mouth the rotten laugh of the fruit-bearing woman sounded. Full blown from now on, now I knew everything. I carried myself. I grew tired from the carrying, I could no longer, I pulsated from inside, I became more and more. How I sat on the beach lost in dreams and played with my shells, my black shell and my white shell. How nice the other women were to me. How they looked after me, like a trinket. The time I coughed so nastily, one of them went specially to the market women to buy bush willow roots, which she could luckily get, and gave me an infusion to drink. And if I complained of the slightest headache I was made to swallow a brew of horn-pod leaves and they said it was good for stomachache too, since the head caught it from the stomach. Well cared for and ringed around and protected and words became knowable and I felt happy but too clumsy, and I felt everyone had to get out of my way.

No one could or would tell me to whom I called when the child's skull made its appearance out of me. It was a scream back to my place of birth. There it echoed. There it echoes.

My baby was so greedy. He had only to say *ee* and I fed him. Soon he was almost too heavy for me to carry. To my owner I no longer existed. Already there was another little thing in my place. I did not speak to her.

I was sold off a second time on the square near the sea where even then the raggedy castor-oil trees were standing. Was sold second-hand. I was a damaged plaything, my bundle of baby and myself bid for separately and disposed of separately. Simply playthings. Useful, certainly. My owner thought he had wasted his money. Someone unknown grabbed my child. What was spoiled? Another examined my head, the inside of my mouth, my pelvis, my arms and legs. He was dubious. What was skew? A merchant sent an agent to buy as many slaves as the fingers of one hand. Where did it leak? Where was it cracked? What was botched about it? The sun baked down on my head. I wanted to faint. Items of everyday use of feminine and masculine gender. One by one. I was left. On one leg. On the other leg. Biting my nails. What was missing? What had been twisted? I no longer saw my child. I spun around. Nothing to see. I screamed within myself. If I could cut open my belly, draw out my guts. I looked for a knife. If I could spit myself out of myself. My heart froze. Who was buying me?

Hateful one. You are loathing like me. Come and kindle your ill in me. I am evil and dangerous. I am dried-out ape dugs and fresh slippery ox eye and peeled-off human skin and the venom of the deadly sea slug with the sucker mouth. I am hatred and hatred's mask. I am deformed. There is a snake in my blood. I drink my own blood. I kick in my swoon. I flounder.

Men came and sang like girls to lay the spirits, but the fires would not flare up. Timbila players from all over the city gathered around me in a circle of clinking slats whose water sounds, sounds like water stars, star drops, dew of bitter stars, were supposed to cool me and, sprinkling down, extinguish my rebellion. But what was I if I was no longer my child? How could an afflicted person feel regret?

Finally the gora player. Tap the single string, a flow of thoughtful sounds gradually moving down the string, a continuous tapping of sounds, each of which immediately fell to earth and became sand and remained lying in the sand never to germinate. Down and down slipped the sounds, deep into the sand. Deeper than taproots ever go.

Deeper than the kingdom of the earthworms. It was enough. It was buried. It was done. I was picked up and, apparently for a risible sum, disposed of. The gora player stopped playing, pushed the stick into his thong belt, put the gora over his shoulder, and left.

That day my new owner bought a glittering cock with bright yellow feathers on head and throat, the neck purple-brown, the back impressively speckled yellow-brown, the wings magnificently black-green with rust-colored tips, the breast a glitter of dark grey and green-gold, a cock with a kick and a crow, and me.

The cock walked around the yard as he wished and mounted the hens whenever he wished. He crowed us awake in the mornings but also crowed in the evenings to predict good weather, upon which it poured. We threatened him with the pot. Cock, cock, we want to eat you. Cock, cock, fly onto the roof ridge of our hut and crow the day red. Your owner is stingy with his chickens. I mean our mutual owner. You and we, cock, cock, your crowing and shitting and our chatting and our excretions and secretions, our babies, our ornaments of pod mahogany seeds and our body cloths, and the house and the warehouse full of baskets of spices and the rats there, all his. The cooking equipment, the eating utensils, our lice, the cockroaches, the ants in the cracks of the walls and the earth around the house, all his. My labor his. My sleep his. My coming and my going. My sweat. My hair. The soles of my feet. The ant can hide away. So can the cockroach. And the rat. Not I. I do not know where. You and I, cock, we are trapped.

When I was expecting my third, I visited an abortionist. My friend stopped me. Life is cheating me, life is poison honey, I complained tiredly. She threw away the seductively scented violet tree roots I had bought.

What did you pay with? she asked.

With myself.

She scolded me. Whore, she called me, which made me laugh.

If it were true I'd be rich.

Go away! she scolded.

Yes, I joked tetchily: the world stretches as far as the master's eye can see.

One day. Oh yes, one day. As far as the master's eye can see, but I wanted to go still further. One day.

My next benefactor-owner plainly had a wider worldview, stretching from deep in the bush to the sea's horizon, including negotiations with gold-miners and woodcutters and the dispatch of goods up the coast and, through the intervention of the charming stranger to whom I, an impudent slave girl, became enslaved, to lands over the sea as well.

It was far, but I wanted still further. I had a craving for distance.

Here now in my baobab I am still bounded on all sides by the horizon. So does one ever break through a horizon? Life is treacherous, like poison honey. Come from afar, I thought I should perhaps pack all the landscapes that had passed before my eyes in a ring around me, that would certainly yield a wider horizon. The further I traveled, the wider it had to become. And in fact everything has shrunk to what a tree defines.

Here there is standstill. Here there are hollowness and artefacts. Here there is care – I hesitate to call it adoration – on the part of the little people who pretend they are invisible. Here there are gifts of venison and sour plums and edible fungus. My ostrich eggshell with the neat little hole breaks and is replaced. My collection of beads is added to. I acquire clothes. I feel good, I feel presentable in my leather apron and cloak decorated with spring-hares' bones, in my self-strung black and green beads and my long strings of ostrich eggshell chips. They are the clothes of a new life in which I travel all around the baobab and never lose sight of it, since what lies on the road back happened only once, and what lies in whatever direction on the other side is (bitter realization) not intended for me to tackle on my own.

I am a melancholic but I do not stop searching, said my ever-voyaging, ever-traveling, my always charming stranger when the eldest son made him the offer. I like to reconnoiter. I like to discover. I cannot get enthusiastic about humanity, but I do not stop testing and do not stop searching.

No, let me not curse him. He should have known that I had no choice but to follow him, for I was not a searcher, I was one driven from circumstance to circumstance, and whoever bought me had to keep me, and this time would keep me. Sometimes it was pleasantly advantageous and easy to be property. I was simply someone together with someone else.

Even before the death of the youngest son, the eldest son had conceived the fantastical plan and begun making arrangements for a brand new kind of expedition. No one had ever heard of such a thing, and our city dwellers were not uninformed. News from across the seas and from the interior reached them regularly. As wide-awake traders they were skeptical about whatever was supported by nothing but guesswork and whatever was, in their considered opinion, the idle talk of poets. The dream of the unknown. The enticement of the foreign. Playing games with knowledge. For such purposes the city had its marginal figures, the subtle word artists and the storytellers on the squares to whom the children listen open-mouthed and whose entertainment value, including the word artists', rose and fell according to whether they succeeded in exciting or boring listener and reader. Yes, they, the colorful madmen. And if a rich man's heir wanted to act stupidly romantic, wanted to prove that an overland route ought to exist, then it meant that there would be opportunities for preying in his absence. It meant that the trade contacts so carefully initiated and forged by his father could now freely be grabbed and taken over by whoever was sly and quick enough. No one expected competition from the middle son, seeing that he had long since settled into a remarkably profitable brothel enterprise behind the glitter and show of the gold-trading business that he had already begun to manage several seasons before the father's death.

And then there was the unfortunate accident to the youngest son, the carefree one. So many disasters struck this house. On the death of his father there followed the quarrel between the eldest son and the spiteful unmarried daughter. She left the family home fuming. Now her dried-out spirit nourished itself on thoughts of vengeance. They swelled up her whole existence from early in the morning till late at night as she intrigued and schemed to bring the eldest son to his knees, even if it meant that she and the married sisters and her two brothers should all go under. She had the look of someone on the hunt. She had the smell of someone who had become cancerous, and whatever she came in contact with she polluted with the venom and the cunning in her breath. She was contaminated with bitterness.

I stayed out of the way of her breath and attached myself with softening heart to the youngest son, to whom I had been bequeathed. He was good and kind and not interested in the slightest in the slaves and slave girls and the other duties he had inherited, and went his way unperturbed with an engaging smile and a casual greeting.

No, I did not believe the stories that he sought out his death because of a disappointment in love. Someone who knew the way through the coral reef as well as he did does not simply stumble, so whispered the slaves to each other, and the mourners in the house. Two fatalities between new moon and full moon. How long is the life of a man? From one wink to another of the lightning. From the fuller swelling of the drop to its fall. So long is the life of man. From move to check-mate. And heads were shaken and hands were wrung – yes, so long *is* life. And the young tree was chopped down, and the voyage was short and the boat capsized and sank, and the mourners piously got through with all such nonsense as befitted the occasion.

No, he was not the type who willfully stepped on a stonefish. Perhaps one of his comrades called his name to draw his attention to a school of rabbitfish in the purple deep-sea water beyond the reef, and he looked up and staggered on a sharp coral point and lost his balance. That was more likely. That, too, was what his comrades said. They brought him home on a stretcher, in his death as slender and beautiful as he was when he left the house in the morning to go and catch fish in that remote bay. Helplessly they had had to watch how, after they had carried him back to the beach, he had thrown himself down without control and kicked, and how foam had come from his mouth, and how he had then grown still, glorious again after the brief mad interlude that had helped him from life to death, again in death as perfect and untouched as he had been in life, a youth who was contained in himself, I reckon, and in his self-absorbed charm had never experienced either sincere friendship or sworn enmity.

I counted up what I stood to lose by his death and what I stood to gain. For the umpteenth time my future was being decided on a whim. I waited tensely. For I knew this fear. Were he and I not old friends? If anyone was ever true to me, then it was he, perhaps because he had become part of me and accompanied my heartbeats as he accompanied my breathing, because he sat in the white of my eye, in the trembling of my fingers. My companion, who had come to acquaint himself with me on my forced march, who had openly made himself at home alongside me and blown his suffocating breath over me – here he was again.

The day after my benefactor's death, when I, soggy with love and confused, had gone in search of the stranger, then too the fear was with me, and it was fear and longing that propelled me forward; and uncertainty, the only certainty I could always count on, led me to streets where mold made the walls break out in multicolored sores and the gates hung askew and rotten and I recognized a building, I recognized some of the slaves who went in and out there with baskets on their backs. It was my previous owner's spice warehouse and I decided to visit my girlfriend, and I arrived in my splendid silk robe and my new quick way of talking, my precious manners, and there I stood awkward with embarrassment, confined within my affectations.

She sat with her legs crossed on the ground in front of the dilapidated hut scratching in the sand with a stick. The hens and chicks scoured as before in the yard, around the huts and house, and around the mango trees where fallen fruit stank sourly. She did not seem to mind the chicken shit and the filth. A naked baby with snotsmears on its top lip crept about on one side and stuck filthy sand into its mouth. I asked if it was hers. She did not reply. She gazed at me. I wanted to pick up the baby but thought better of it. I considered what I could give him. My friend gazed at me. When I walked off, I felt that piercing gaze on me. I felt someone throw something that hit me. I turned around. I saw her picking up handfuls of sand and throwing them at me. I called her name. The baby, also hit by the sand, laughed with delight. Then he began to cry. I walked off, overcome. The baby cried with rage.

I went back past the slaughterhouse and the tall palm trees there that tried not to see anything. I walked past the market women and the slave square and the skiffs drawn up on the beach, their masts snapped back like comical antennae. I saw the sole dhow frisking on the swell and called out again my shrill inquiry about the stranger and saw again gestures saying no, and I turned back to the great dreary silent house where bundles of jasmine bulged over the garden walls and put their scent in service of the dead.

How did my benefactor come by his wealth? I once asked the stranger, when he and I were all that remained. I stroked the pea-shaped swellings of the scarification marks on his forehead. My finger glided over them. Two mad pioneers that we had become, now two devoted to each other.

How? I asked again in the intervals between a lourie's abuse. My finger glided over his lips, purple as a fig. How thin he had become, it struck me. His cheeks so sunken. He lay with eyes closed in a hollow full of soft moldering leaves.

Busybody, he tried to hush me. I kept on asking.

Your kind made him the most powerful person in the city, the stranger then said. You ought to feel flattered, actually. Your benefactor was a connoisseur in a class of his own and seldom bought lower-grade material. In your case he was absolutely right. Look, he indicated, your physical proportions are of a rare symmetry.

He wanted to stroke me. I pulled my arm away.

How did he come by his wealth?

Again the stranger came with evasive explanations of aesthetic considerations that had led the benefactor-merchant to seek perfection, a balance between beautiful externals and the intrinsic, and that had also led him to view his slaves as a collection of art objects, meticulously purchased with an eye to investment and sometimes disposed of individually at a profit after he had refined them through education, as he had admittedly done in my case. It was then pointed out to me that my benefactor had displayed a remarkable appreciation of my qualities, to such an extent that he had never disposed of me and even allowed me at his deathbed.

That's not how he got rich, I objected. He must already have had a lot of money to afford such a hobby. Where did this man come by the means for it?

And what if I said he was a brigand?

Then that is what he was.

A slave raider?

Everyone is a robber of something. Robbers are all I know.

Am I one?

How should I know?

What if I were?

Then you are.

I rob money, I don't rob people, said the stranger. I rob on the open seas. I rob before I am robbed, before I become booty.

Like me, I said.

Yes.

Did my benefactor hunt us in the interior?

No, the stranger laughed, that is not how one becomes rich. The outlay is not worth the trouble and the profit. Rather be an ivory hunter, for your product is something dead, more easily transported. People, on the other hand, die like flies, and have to be fed, and try to escape, and your expenditure on guards, on food, on weapons, is tremendous. Human loss is comparable to capital loss. No, it is the exceptional type who becomes a slave hunter. And then you run the danger too of being killed and robbed in turn. That is how your benefactor set to work. He had spies everywhere, and messengers. Then he ambushed the slave raiders and their convoys somewhere near the coast, when all of them, captives and guards, were tired to death and offered little resistance. That was when he was young. He put together enough to build his house, where he could live peacefully as an established prominent citizen, turned his back on brigandage, and concentrated on gold, ambergris and wood, on copper, to which the rich people of the city attached more value than gold, and on his hobby.

Then the stranger lay with his eyes shut, silent, as though exhausted by talking.

I felt helpless with humiliation but tried not to cry, or not to cry visibly or audibly. Possession and loving are concepts that damn each other. I did not want to be as he and the others, all the others in my life, from my earliest memories of huts and mother and security in a misty, sultry forest basin, from my memories of the lascivious man who bought me to deflower me, and the spice merchant whose labors I had to endure grinding my teeth, I did not want to be as they all regarded me, all of them, my benefactor with his fatherliness and this one too, this man whom I embraced with my whole body and allowed to come into me time after time so as to be absolutely full of him, absolutely convulsively full and rich and fulfilled, floating, seed satisfied, making him, self-content, part of me, of me exclusively – he too, he who had just described me analytically and disposed of me like an object in a dispensation, even he, I was different from what they all thought, utterly different from what anyone might think, I rejected all the opinions, all the observations and reprimands of all the women in my life, what did they know of who I was, what did any of them know.

I remembered the poets' sarcastic remarks about women in general, but at the time I had not taken them to heart: to tell the truth, I joined in the so-called sophisticated disparagement, and this kind of superficial display of lust did not strike me as vile and immediately to be condemned. Vain. Vainly and frivolously I participated. Clothed in luxurious fabric that enveloped me like a soft caress and with saffian sandals on my feet, quickly adept in all the little arts of seduction, I joined in the talk and laughter. I felt, I knew I was in my flower. I laughed without reserve. I sent laughter upward and outward and picked myself the pale purple double stars of the wild chestnut blossoms to stick in my hair.

My benefactor smiled. He found it attractive. When I put my arms around him it was like protecting a child. Crazy, when he was the possessor, but it was so. He propped his head against my shoulder like, and with the innocence of, a child. And in the wink of an eye he changed and became wiser than I, scolded me, took over and initiated the caresses, and when we had intercourse he was both father and son and I mother and trustful daughter. We knew everything together, completely, wishing for nothing more. Until later on he grew so weak, so pathetically emaciated and listless as the fever got the upper hand that he scarcely made his appearance in the dining room any longer but chose to remain lying on cool palm mats in his room. Afternoon rain outdoors, the cool brought on by the evenings and followed in the nights by the sharp sparkling of stars as a bonus, the white splash of moonlight over him – all this did little to change his state of mind. In every corner of the room the eye of death glittered. Sometimes he stared absently out over the sea and declined the extract of bitter false-thorn pods that one of us held out to him in a delicate little porcelain bowl. Likewise ignored the prescriptions of the city's best doctors, uttered his thanks laconically in a hoarse voice and made no use of them.

In my perfect arms he died, supported between my perfect thighs, leaning against my perfect breasts, he and I, father, mother, child, owner, valued art object and servant, lovers.

It had happened too long ago to wish to hate him. There was no time to hate anyone and plan revenge. The veld threatened us. I turned back to the stranger whose gentle nature I had also found out about on this interminably long journey to the mirage of a city in a blooming red desert. Where I had earlier allowed myself to be charmed by his wit, I learned during this time to appreciate his humanity and helpfulness. The circumstances were certainly not conducive to deep conversations embroidered with light-hearted thesis and antithesis, and in those days it seldom happened that the two of us spoke together. I think the encircling silence was too great. It compelled our respect. No, it is silly to think so, for in truth we were usually too tired to begin a conversation. I could not deny that things were going badly for us.

We shuffled one behind the other through the hot region, our tired gaze measured the distance to the next spot of coolness and the relief of a roof of leaves, and though we knew we could not afford it, we lingered longer and longer in this way in the shadows of trees. Like now.

We exchanged apologetic looks. I took his hand and pressed his fingers to my mouth.

We had to be going. It was no good. We had to make up our minds. We thought of the alluring city and everything that would be awaiting us there. We filled in the scanty information provided by the hunters with our imagination, and the deeper we went into the interior, the further from home, the more desolate the bush and the slower and more unwilling our bodies, the more richly we festooned the images we had called up. We did not see that we had begun to pretend that what we wanted must exist. We referred to the city as if it were an accomplished fact that we would soon reach it, just another day and another day, just another couple of days and another couple of days, then we would see it lying on the horizon, flat and shining at the foot of mountains consisting of pure rose quartz.

I dreamed of that rose quartz. My dreams were stuffed full of rose quartz. I could barely move among the craggy pieces. The floors of my dreams were rose quartz, the pillars and the ceiling of my dreams. I peered out between the rose quartz at the rest of the world. I withdrew into rose quartz and nodded contentedly.

But first we had to cross the swamp, the hunters had said.

The more burningly I longed to see the city at the foot of the rose quartz mountains, the longer I wanted to postpone the sight of the swamp between. For I did not believe the description of white and green water lilies arranged on dew-clear water wherever you looked, and golden reeds to which the tiniest red and silver painted frogs clung, and spiders that tumbled from the glitter of their webs when the dugouts bent the grass.

I had seen what a swamp looked like when we left the sea behind. I felt its oppressive air upon me and its sharp smell irritated my nostrils. Its endless green expanse stretching into the haze enclosed me. I heard a sucking and a bubbling and saw the snouts of crocodiles lying in the bruised mud. I saw mosquitoes in a mist above the pools. I saw mudskippers creep halfway out to stare boldly at me. And the worst was the silence that I vaguely recognized from earlier on. It was the oppressiveness that had been lying in wait for me on a journey of horror so long ago I should scarcely have been able to report on it. But I recognized this silence. It was the supreme wide silence that prevailed over the noisy croaking of the frogs. The silence had a width of weight that muted your appetite for life and then after a never-ending day tried to press you into the mud and bury you with the wingbeat of night. Was it the immeasurability that made yellow sweat drops burst out on your forehead and disturbed your breathing? I recognized it. There was also fear, a sticky fear that shut off your throat. I recognized the fear. In what ways could I still experience it? I knew the fear of bloodthirstiness and of isolation and of ignorance and of punishment and of bewilderment. I knew him.

This fear was part of the air. It hung as far as the coast where the city of my various owners commenced with shanties and pole fences, with herds of untended goats and spill-off channels full of nightsoil, the busy commercial city to which I was kidnapped.

I had already tried to imagine a kind of existence in which I was not a possession, but it did not come easily to me. What would have become of me in the land of my origin? Would I, for example, have walked, sat, stood differently? Would I have entered into other kinds of friendship, accepted wholly different opinions? Would I have clung to religion? Would I have had a husband, and children by him only? Children I would have raised till they could stand on their own feet? Suddenly I thought: I would have been able to be a grandmother. Grandchildren playing around me in a yard full of tame guineafowl.

Suddenly I saw: here in this city I would never become a grand-mother. Here I functioned as a mother till my children were as high as my hip, then I lost all say over them. They disappeared from my life. For me there was no continuation, no links backwards or forwards. There was coming and ending, a finality as if darkness were made abiding. If it had been death, I would have had certainty. Now I did not know.

Where were the children I had brought into life? How would I be able to recognize them if I bumped into them somewhere? And would I be able to recognize them? Sometimes I looked attentively at young faces, searched for myself in their features, their voices, their behavior, their posture – assuming that my children were all here, I thought bit-terly, and not sold into service in other cities and countries. I wondered whether I would be able to pick out a child of my own by maternal feeling, no matter where or how we met. Would I know it was he? Would I immediately feel a glow of recognition course through me, and yearn to press him to me, meticulous identification having been rendered unnecessary by a bittersweet knowledge within me, a source of certainty warmer than the sun, like mothers are supposed to have? Mothers being unfathomable, after all.

It had not yet happened. Nor had I yet heard of such cases. But I continued to look into young faces, listen to young talk.

In the house of my benefactor it was part of my duties to amuse his grandchildren when his married daughters or his middle son paid visits with their spouses and children. Such visits occurred often, at any time, unannounced, and I enjoyed the fun. I liked to see the little ones gobble down sweets. I liked it when they clambered up and over me tirelessly, and I liked telling stories; but with the older boys and girls I did not get along as well. I felt strangely embarrassed with them. It was as if I had consciously to sense their attitudes and desires, and as if my lack of intuition were noticeable in my behavior, as if I betrayed my confusion, even as if I were afraid that they would detect a flaw in me which excessive friendliness and affability simply could not disguise. So there remained a distance between us. Fortunately some of them were already provided with their own slave or slave girl to see specifically to their needs, while the slave girls who came along to look after the small children were only too ready to leave the work and fuss to me. And I enjoyed it. I enjoyed wiping dirty little mouths and listening to terrible accusations and finding words of comfort for little hurts and big frights. Hey! Hey! I called – Don't put finger into the parrot's cage! Oh no! And I cuddled the little bodies till they were out of breath with delighted laughter.

I felt uneasy when my benefactor caught me doing this. His smile. It did not at all rhyme with the self I tried to be for him, and it was certainly not good for my self-confidence in his bedroom. Abruptly I stopped playing and waited, hanging my head, for him to go.

On the whole I could not complain about my place and the scope given to me in his household. I considered myself a lucky, privileged person, without rights but not wholly without choice. Not all slaves by far were as well cared for as those of this house, as I could attest from experience. Granted, we slept in an outside building, but it was built of stone like the main house. Our floors were not covered with carpets. We slept on thick coir mats. There were no ornately carved low tables and red-copper urns standing about in our rooms. But compared with the slovenliness and stuffiness and sour mud and the holes in the wind-torn roof of my previous owner's slave huts, I could certainly consider myself lucky. Add to this my privileged position which I knew very well how to maintain, and the spick-and-span organization of the house, and I really had little to grumble about.

On the terrace roof where, thanks to my position as favorite, I could freely repair without permission, I liked to spend the sunset, when I could fit it in. At such times I would look at the glow over the interior out of the cloudy fierceness of which I had come, and on the opposite side at the darkening sea that had called me, and I would stand caught in perfect balance in the interlight. In inescapable transitoriness I could have dissolved like a phantom into the swift black. I was marked out in peacefulness, and whole. When a dog barked, I started out of my rumination and breathed deeply, salty air, smell of crayfish, smell of damask rose, smell of clove and broadbean. I could smell the first early stars. For that reason I could not understand why I might not keep my children. For that reason I had to accept that grown children were what I lacked.

For that reason I felt relieved that I had not yet fallen pregnant again.

And thankful that I did not belong to the eldest son, whose nature was so utterly different from his father's, for the stories of maltreatment were not just stories. I myself had seen the open raw weals on the shoulders of some of his slaves, and had stealthily nursed them. It was as if the eldest son took out his annoyance on men in particular – in fact he had no slave girls. Not that he would find need for them in his father's house, but still I thought it strange. We, the slave girls, scarcely existed for this surly young man with his cane eternally in his hand. He had a blunt way of talking to us when he really had to, for example when he had to ask one of us to pass a dish at table, and he did not partake in the amusing man-to-woman pleasantries of the writers. He sat there shyly, half-leaning on a cushion, nibbling, and all that really animated him was talk about the history of other countries. Then his eyes glowed beneath the thin line of his eyebrows. And then he closed his eyes. The eyelids looked defenseless with their short curly lashes when his face relaxed so unexpectedly, and like a child he scratched in his ear with his little finger, and shook his head, and his eyes opened in a stare.

A good thing I had so little to do with him. To me he seemed clumsy, closed off. A good thing I could never have dreamed I would one day spend such a long stretch of my life in his company: and even after that, after he had shamefully abandoned us and taken along everything left over, even after that I could not fathom him. He had a habit of bumping the slaves, or tripping them and grinning when they fell with a heavy pack of provisions. Maliciously he beat the sanga cattle till the stranger intervened and virtually came to blows with him and wrestled with him. He made me shudder. Whether he left me alone because slave girls scarcely existed for him, or whether he did not dare assault me because I was at the time the stranger's property, I did not know. Do not know even now. I felt protected in the company of my stranger.

Distracted with despondency, I accosted the stranger the first time he came after the youngest son's death and begged him to buy me before I was disposed of at the market. That is what I feared would happen to me, that I would again have to go and stand in that place of shame. I remember how I gestured hysterically, how shrill my voice sounded, and later how tremulous; then I shut up. Too anguished, too tired out by struggling in the grip of uncertainty. Overconscious of being obtrusive, rash. The short interval before he answered was laden with my intensity, my violent beseechings were an indecorous wrangling with his reserve, my clammily waving hands helpless feelers before his face, my kneeling attitude a too obviously toadying trick.

When he assured me I would not be auctioned off, how lovely the flash of transition from uncomprehended relief at first to comprehension and calm. I brought a corner of my garment to my mouth to stifle my indecorously unrestrained sobs, and, to all appearances calmly thanked him while choking on my feelings and wanting to scream and rejoice crazily. Subdued I left him.

For he came again as I believed he would; but this time there was a motive I could not guess, for I assumed without thinking that he had come to do his everyday business, come to buy up iron and copper in exchange for rolls of silk and cotton, come on the trade wind at the head of the little fleet of dhows under his command as of old, come from afar across the rippling blue-green where other trading cities on other coasts shrouded themselves in a haze of strangeness – that is how I thought. That he and his crew had come to unload one cargo and take on another.

I could not know that this time he would temporarily relinquish his command over the sailors and hand it over to a subordinate in order to undertake a journey in the opposite direction from the white flutter dance of the brown-veined butterflies over mountains and plains, nobody knew whither, nobody knew why. And no one knew why he had allowed himself to be talked into it. He provided no reasons. He went. I accompanied him, his recently acquired latest possession. I became part of the extensive organization that kept him and the eldest son busy and had them doing calculations till late at night by oil lamps and had them unraveling the possible, the probable, the actual and the enigmatic and weighing them up against each other till one grew bored. The possible and the impossible fell, rose and hovered in balance. The particulars heaped up and up, and an idea suffocated, and new ideas were sought, and eventually the question why was of absolutely no importance. Fancy and the profit motive. Childish dreams. Longing for the faraway. Elaborate estimates. A rebellious streak. Perhaps the last.

So. For that reason we departed for the frontiers of the spirit. Invertebrates about to change homes, that is what we were. Shellfish sliding over the sand. A colony of sea anemones slithering over dry rocks on their single feet. Fish walking on their fins. Wobbling salt-scaled coelacanths. Wailing dugongs.

Our procession of bearers and cattle and sedan chairs with passengers on the shoulders of bearers wound into the interior on the way to the great ocean that booms at the uttermost limits of the world. It could not be too far, as determined by the eldest son and the stranger, rationally, with the help of their maps. It could not take a lifetime, they calculated. Taking everything into account, it ought in fact to be a shortcut to the land of the able mariners who had recently called at the city and boasted of their hardships on the billows of an immense unknown sea, and who could prove on the evidence of the numerous cases of scurvy among the crew that they came from the utmost limits of the utmost limits.

To us it seemed as if they suddenly appeared out of nothing, as if they slowly came shifting across the foil of the sea, oh so slowly, in bulky caravels driven by a mass of patched sails in the tackling of which we saw the crew scrambling with apelike agility. We were not impressed. Or did not make it apparent. But in spite of this gathered on the beach or climbed to the terrace roofs. If you were rich you ordered a sedan chair, if you were a perky child you climbed the bow of a coconut tree, if you were a carpenter you dropped your tools and forgot your commissions and stood up, if you had a suspicion of new trade connections you locked up your trading house and with a small retinue of scribes sauntered, calm, chatting, exchanging greetings, pretending boredom, to the spot, more or less, where they would drop anchor in our treacherous bay. What can they offer that we do not have? was the general feeling, and the city did not seethe with excitement, not so that it could be seen, and the new arrivals were nonchalantly made welcome, not suspiciously, but still . . . Not so that it could be seen.

The eldest son was the first to be invited aboard the flagship. He asked the stranger to accompany him because of his greater knowledge of marine matters. I remember how noble the stranger looked in his green-striped robe with green headdress, how he towered above the bearded newcomers as he stood on the commander's deck and he and the eldest son tried to make themselves understood in sailors' language, with plenty of gestures and headshaking, up and down, back and forth. We all waited on the report. We learned about a land at the other end of the earth's disc and about voyagers who had sailed as far as here all along the edge of the world and about the mighty storms with which the gods tried to drive them over the edge and plunge them into nothingness, and about voices they heard in the howling wind warning them to turn around, and about monsters on land where they wanted to fetch fresh water, about short rests to repair broken yards, about beacons they had erected and about hostile backward peoples, and they pointed, so we learned, at a red sign on their yellow sails and explained that they sailed for their king, these stocky hairy men in thick peculiar garments.

Unnoticed as the birth of a wave an idea came into being and swelled unnoticed. The city's richest merchant's as yet unmarried eldest son, he with the interest in far places because of which he felt attracted to the stranger and kept pestering him with his questions, he who now after his father's death had inherited the most important trading interests, this very person hurriedly got married on the eve of his departure for a destination which according to everyone existed only in his imagination and about which he was secretly laughed at.

Only one did not laugh, namely the stranger, whom he persuaded to seal his fate thus: to cease, temporarily, one presumed, voyaging over the high seas from one land mass to another and back, voyaging across a too well-known water mass afflicted with cyclones, blessed with monsoons, and to essay the unknown of a land journey with a vague goal. A gaze accustomed to the nervous riffling of water would have to accustom itself to the green of forest and marsh, to ravines veiled in old man's beard and steep cliffs, to plains and sluggish rivers and a horizon of dome-shaped hills. The stars no longer teemed over an unstable water surface but over the stability of resistant earth, and looked relatively calmer and of surer course in the wide night. The stars of the earth would look stiller. The night look thicker. Everything would look more dependable.

I suppose it was the spirit of adventure. I can't be bothered with what made him embark upon something so silly that would provide him with a trivial death in the heart of the wilderness, lamented by his last possession, myself. I was the only one left to pace up and down the river bank calling anxiously, plaintively, urgently, hopelessly, and to feel mocked by the fish eagles that wove the strip of air above the river from tree to tree with their screeches and proclaimed it forbidden territory by order of the giant crocodile.

Come to his end in the belly of a reptile. There are times when I really can't help laughing at it. It is after all a particularly laughable death. One is so used to regarding other inhabitants of the earth as food, to accepting them, as it were, as self-evident sources of food, and to putting whatever is edible in service of one's digestion, to raising the ingestion of food to an art by adding condiments and tastefully serving up dishes that go together, to making a huge fuss of a meal and to developing customs around it that ossify into rituals, to making a whole rigmarole of the utterly natural bodily function of eating – one is so used to it that it seems terribly funny when other-consuming man is himself eaten. The untouchably mighty, revealed to be nothing but food, was knocked into the water with a well-aimed flick of the tail – actually not well aimed, actually executed with unconscious perfection – and drowned and devoured.

Did his spirit perhaps escape in bubbles? Did my companion the water spirit grow jealous and demand him as hers?

Then I grew afraid of pursuing my thoughts. I who am of water never wished it on him, and however ridiculous, he is no longer among the living, however laughable to be passed out as crocodile manure, as if it were less ridiculous to be buried and eaten by worms. He perished. He is no more.

From then on I thought carefully about the nature of his death, and I thought of it as a normal incident, I disguised it from myself, I concealed the circumstances from myself and I told myself a completely different story. Even when in my loneliness I bitterly cursed him and his nobility, or, as I was to decide, his stubborn rectitude, I used a figure of speech in which the name of my great spirit never appeared. Curse the ground that drank his blood, I preferred to say; trying to expel the abomination into the earth, or I made it stick to hyena and vulture. I brought an offering to the dark hippopotamus pool where the ruler of the crocodiles lived. Solemnly I threw my ivory bracelet in. It sank noiselessly, leaving scarcely a ripple. Harmony was restored and in the silence brought by the wind there was only the screech of the fish eagles, guardians of the stretch of water.

Could I but know whether I too am destined for a watery death! I long for it. Perhaps I had to understand that water would be his fate where he was untrue to the great water by which he lived.

I swear I will be true. Every time I plunge my ostrich eggshell into the bubbling of the stream, I mutter:

> *Water yes water*
> *you live in the reed's bed*

and in the hollow of the baobab
water you come out of the air
water you well up out of the earth
you cover the earth
you live under it and above it
your spirit is as great in a drop
as in flood and storms
eagerly I collect you and drink you
water you are in me

The water in the stream tastes sweet. I am thankful I wandered here after the stranger's disappearance. In humility I thank my water spirit for guiding me. And for the thunderstorms that wash the baobab nice and clean and spur him to bud and all at once thrust out all his leaves and hang up his great flowers one by one on twigs, white and crumpled, to be fertilized by the bats, white, crumpled and malodorous.

When the tree blooms, then I cannot feel somber. Then I see the journey as a confusion I had to undergo, then I do not try to unravel it and make sense of it. I say the name of the tree aloud, the name of water, of air, fire, wind, earth, moon, sun, and all mean what I call them. I say my own name aloud and my own name means nothing. But I still am.

One time I fled from the tree. I ran aimlessly into the veld, trying to get out of its sight by hiding behind a high round rock, and I opened my mouth and brought out a sound that must be the sound of a human being because I am a human being and not a wildebeest that snorts and not a horned locust that produces whistling noises with its wings and not an ostrich that booms, but a human being that talks, and I brought out a sound and produced an accusation and hurled it up at the twilight air. A bloody sound was exposed to the air, with which I tried to subject everything around me. To be able to dominate with one long raw sound.

At night I hear lions roar. Every now and again I get up to throw wood on the fire. Sometimes I see eyes shining greenishly in the firelight. In the mornings I bake tubers that the little people have brought me in the ashes, break open a hard-shelled monkey orange with a stick and scoop the flesh with the stick into my mouth. A gulp of water, baked bulbs, and I am ready to resume my struggle against time. We fight in an endless roundabout circle. I do not manage to divide him up and segment him, so as to form a pattern and control him, in spite of my ingenuity with the beads. I sometimes get confused and forget when I linked what to what. Green and black mixed up in accordance with my mood. I cannot shake time off me. He squats continually before my tree. Everything that has been in my life is always with me, simultaneously, and the events refuse to stand nicely one after the other in a row. They hook into each other, shift around, scatter, force themselves on me or try to slop out of my memory. I have difficulty with them in the necklace of my memory. I am not a carefree little herder of time at all. Day and night pass. Summer and winter, another summer, and here is winter again. This is easy, but not the time that had made of me what I am and that lives within me with another rhythm.

Sometimes when I am washing myself in the river I regard my reflection critically in a calm pool and try to determine how much older I have become. It is not easy, for however motionless both I and the water are, there is a continual fine wrinkling distortion of my image, a water wrinkle that flatteringly replaces the possible wrinkling of age. I throw a pebble into myself. I rock grotesquely up and down and break up in lumps. Restless I. Then I withdraw myself from my divided self in the water. How my spirit struggles. I bake myself dry in the sun, dress, and take the path up to my dwelling. Soon the elephants will arrive. The sun already hangs in the baobab's arms.

At times simply melancholy.

I do not follow the little people's click language. It sounds to me just as if geckos have begun talking. Anyhow, how could I learn it? After that strange first near-meeting they seldom speak within hearing distance of me. One day I saw them bring down a giraffe. While they were flaying the animal and cutting it open they babbled excitedly, even quarreled, so it seemed to me. I listened attentively but learned nothing. It is a language for geckos and tapping beetles.

Out of respect I stand in such a position in the opening of the baobab that they do not see me. After the time when I forced them to look at me and saw how it offended them, I never force myself on them any more, and accept with gratitude and joy every crumb of food they bring and every object of use.

And every useless object. Like the handful of little gold nails. How they shine. How pretty. I already have beads, sherds, an ostrich egg-shell, clothes, and, wonder of wonders, a whole clay pot black with age but still perfectly usable that the little people found and brought to me and with which I transport water on my head. And now these lovely playthings.

I let my thoughts roam and imagine the most wonderful history of a town with bulging walls and stones packed in chevrons, of a holy echo that delivers oracles in a roar over the veld. A town more or less like the one we saw the women on our travels building. In fact we passed several such stone towns. Some abandoned and disintegrating, some half-finished and left just like that to become rubble, some in the process of being built. Walls to prop terraces and walls for houses or temples or barns, all erected by the labor of women. There was not a man to be seen anywhere, which as a matter of fact seemed strange to me.

But perhaps the men were out hunting. Are they out hunting? I asked the stranger over my shoulder.

I think so, he answered.

Do the women always build alone? Do they always carry the stones themselves, do they always pack them themselves, do they draw up the plans themselves?

Strange, strange, answered the stranger.

From the sedan chairs that carried us swinging from side to side past them, we regarded these zealous women workers curiously. I held a big leaf over my eyes to keep the sun off. Like a real lady I sat and watched the multitude laboring in the scorching sun, and made remarks and observations in a light, contented mood, I felt so good. Never before had life been so pleasant.

Perhaps the men are out at war. Perhaps they are planning an attack on us, joked the stranger.

What does our leader say? I asked.

Oh, he's always in a bad temper. He is too intense.

Yes.

I felt myself to be a peculiarly elevated, untouchable, temporary spectator always on the move, and thought out something else pithy to utter from my seat. Perhaps they are . . . I wanted to say slave women. I choked the word down.

Perhaps among them were some of my unknown family members who had remained behind. Perhaps I came from here, or from near by. It was wiser not to ask questions and to let things pass. Or were the men perhaps out on a slave raid, and must the women do the men's work? The women were bare from the waist up. They wore snail shells and multicolored amulets decorated with beads around their necks and ankle rings of copper wire. So I rode on in perfect privilege, in the security of being preferred, in the status lent to me on this trip by virtue of being the select maidservant of one of the leaders. No, not the maidservant, not at all – the mistress. I had the freedom of finding myself in strange parts with a man on whom I could have doted and a crowd of servants and a surly leader, but him I easily forgot. And no chance of escaping. To throw myself on the mercy of the inhospitable? How foolish that would be. Foolish even to want to make contact with these women when no sure welcome was guaranteed to me and help would not necessarily be offered. So I swung on haughtily but eager-eyed past the brown stone walls in the green grass. No right angles here but soft curves connecting with the earth's curves. Thus women build.

For a while I had been noticing something in my front bearer's hair. Now I saw he was keeping cross money coins there. Stolen money, therefore. Tonight I would warn him to hide it better, for the bearers were continually changed to spread the burdens better. Before long he would have to help carry the eldest son and it was to be doubted whether the latter would let such a glaring offense pass unpunished. Poor devil. Did he want to run away one day? Did he want to flee one night, and in his flight call at villages to buy food? Did he want to take to his heels, his head heavy with metal, his heart light with rejoicing, his insides hollow with fear?

In fact, he was our first loss. Apparently he managed to disappear. Our second loss was a much more telling blow. The beautiful gentle sanga cattle disappeared overnight as if an earth spirit had made a cavern open and one by one they had all walked in, and now stood lowing in the belly of the earth and clashing their long horns and tramping miserably around.

We found that we had posted no sentries for the night, since we had never done so. We also found that we had no tracker in service, and we ourselves spotted nothing in the rain-polished veld, just our own muddy prints, traces of frivolousness, proofs of ignorance tramped far and wide.

It was a serious loss. Not only had the cattle carried the heaviest packs, but they were a last resort if hunger were to stare us in the face, and in addition it had been our intention to exchange them with tribes of the interior, in case of need, for food or information or, if need be, protection. That was how it had been planned.

The first quarrel between the leaders of the expedition resulted in uneasy silence. A momentary display of indignation, a knife-grinding of reproaches, and both withdrew from the conflict impatient and dissatisfied and stalked around as if a glittering crane crest of aggrievedness were tightly settled on their heads, and their stiff faces betrayed no desire to be reconciled. Stubborn, arrogant, could not sit still so long. A sailor is always on his feet, always on the go. The sea, his road, never rests. It pushes you, pulls you, whisks you up and down, throws you to port, to starboard, it splashes against you, sweeps past you, it takes its form in accord with its whims, it comes rolling mountain high, it becomes a whirlpool and spins you in a deep blue vortex, it stretches itself out flat and holds you imprisoned on its calm green mood, it changes and remains the same in its changing and makes of change a permanence and of unpredictability the only predictability. It is not fickle, it is always thus. And therefore he preferred to walk, the stranger explained, mocking himself. In brief, he had neither rest nor peace. In brief, he walked to make the slaves' work easier.

I too, some days, usually in the early mornings. My garment drew a wet trail in the dew. There was faint daybreak to give light. I tried to catch up with my long long shadow with greater and greater steps. To be able to walk on my head. I never catch up with myself, I sighed happily. Birds whirred up from the grass. I noted: a steenbuck skipping away – whizz, gone; a troop of redbuck ruminating expressionlessly; a white rhinoceros bull, firm as a rock; a restless red jackal; and a lion with caked mane and flies around its snout yawning the yawn of the satiated and rolling over comically. Till the sun made its nest in my back – then I beckoned the bearers nearer.

Long ago abandoned trying to hold a conversation with them. My requests were fulfilled in silence. No answers. No questions. It was like trying to get through to zombies. More than in the city where I necessarily had to work with this type, it struck me here in untouched nature how inhumanly they were behaving. Whether unwilling or to appearances obliging, their actions were those of fellows of the tikoloshe-spirit, it occurred to me. Their eyes were peculiarly empty, their motions automatic as if they were obeying built-in commands.

We have people bewitched among us, I whispered to the stranger. Didn't you notice it before?

I stared at him in surprise. We were relaxing in the heat of noon under a splendid cucumber tree on the bank of a full river. The eldest son had gone for a walk, as usual without mentioning it to us, without saying where he was going; he would probably reveal nothing when he came back. And we two, we felt too happy in each other's presence to care about his morbid reserve, we two were a self-sufficiency and, jealously eager for each other's attention, let the sourpuss go his way.

We had just finished eating what the slaves had prepared for us. Had it not been for the handfuls of flying ants that one of them had collected the previous night and turned into a tolerable sauce, we would have had to choke down the thick millet porridge just like that. As we had been doing for several days. For with the disappearance (or was it the theft?) of the cattle and the redistribution of the packs, some of the goods had of necessity to be left behind, and thus, by mistake, we had to assume, the rice, the dried shrimps, the mango chutney, the dried fig cakes, the coconuts, the dates and much else was left behind. There were no accusations of carelessness thrown back and forth, but to discord smoldered. One leader formed the vanguard, the other leader and I the rearguard, and we were separated by mistrust and by a train of slaves.

Sugarbirds clung to the bunches of purple-red flowers that displayed themselves above our heads. There was a languid cooing of doves. A virtual stasis reigned. Water shining among plumed reeds. A caressing breeze. I am listening, I said. Tell.

At night I call all my familiar spirits, whispered the stranger, pretending to be mysterious. Have you not yet heard the hyena snuffling? Just as well you sleep so deeply. Have you not yet heard the faraway bark of the baboon?

Have you not yet seen the aardvark's hump stand out against the moonlight and the long snout with which he sniffs out the corpses? Poor inhabitants of the villages along our route, they don't know what hits them. They have no knowledge of wizards who make an appearance now here now there and make their familiars violate their graves. Have you not yet seen the eyes shining in the night, eyes red as fire, half-eyes, squint eyes? Have you not yet heard the growling and the scrabbling and the shuffling, and the cracking of bones? I send my familiars into the kraals to the graves of the chieftains. The cattle are too terrified to low. They stand aside. The next day the cows drop calves with two heads and the golden-red acres of millet through which the familiars galloped with their enchanted riders lie flattened and cannot be harvested, and the great famine comes to all the regions through which we travel. The storage baskets are emptied. The livestock die. People look at one another with eyes red as fire, with half-eyes, with squint eyes, and fall upon the weak and eat them up. They cut off their lips and fingertips, they let them bleed to death in pots of water, cook them and eat them up, the tastiest bits for the strongest, the offal and the gravy for what children remain.

The stranger went and lay flat on his back and stared up through the latticework of branches and dark green insets of foliage to the tatters of blue sky.

Pretty stories, he said. He supported his head on his hands. I have tried to live, he said, without religion and other such superstitions, without escapism of any kind, and now I find myself in the greatest illusion of my life. Now I seek consolation in shortsightedness and look no further than the night of every day.

There followed a mumbled rumination that I could not follow properly. I thought I heard him ask me for forgiveness. He stopped the mumbling. He sat up and looked at me narrowly.

I shall have to live the story out to its end, he decided. All stories end. For a moment he was still, his attention drawn by a swarm of starlings flying round and round the cucumber tree.

All I know is that I wanted to, he said sharply, as if answering an unuttered question of mine. I wanted to. Then he added, with the slightest trace of a smile in the furrows at the corners of his mouth and in the narrowing of his eyes: I think one can be ridiculous with dignity. Or try to.

Something broke through the underbrush on our left. Flapping, waving and shouting with fear the eldest son came racing towards us, stumbled like a clown and slipped over the tussocks of grass. The hem of his clothes caught on a num-num bush and held him back; jerking and pulling desperately, beating the bush flat with his cane, he tried angrily to rid himself of the thorns' grip, but only got further entangled, and eventually had to tear his clothes free. All the while he hoarsely commanded us and the slaves to fall flat, to hide, to crouch, to creep away, to make ourselves scarce.

Instead of making ourselves scarce we all stood up straight and gazed dumbstruck at the spectacle. With a muffled curse he freed himself from the num-num thorns and stamped over to us and explained that there was an army on the way, on the river.

Fall flat! Fall flat! he exhorted us panting. He must have run quite a distance in the hot sun.

He himself fell to his knees behind the dense reeds and hushed as if in prayer. I considered whether to follow his example. The stranger and I exchanged amused looks, though no longer exactly beaming with self-confidence and boldness, and when one of the slaves silently gestured that he saw something coming, we did indeed fall flat with our noses to the ground, each on the spot where he had stood.

I managed to turn my head carefully to one side and peer at the river, but detected nothing as yet. The plumes arched so calmly. The waterfowl had not let themselves be alarmed. I could see brown ducks drifting in the shallow water and also a giant heron's motionless head and neck sticking out above the reeds, and as I lifted my face slightly higher I saw the tense blue hovering tremor of a kingfisher at diving distance above the water and could also see the far bank walled off from the veld by a rampart of fully grown wild figs.

My ears helped me. I heard the thump of oars and concentrated on listening very carefully. I thought I could recognize human voices. Tatters of speech came to us where we lay quiet as wild animals, waiting for danger to pass. Later I saw through jagged cracks in the reeds several hollowed-out tree trunks sailing past in pairs in a kind of formation from left to right, each with a team of rowers rowing upstream with great effort. The oars came up dripping and sank rhythmically. Their progress was very leisurely. Probably the speed of the current was badly against them here. In about the middle of the formation one hollowed-out tree trunk larger than the rest glided past alone, with, it seemed to me, a larger crew wearing tufts of animal tails around their upper arms, and in the stern there seemed to be a kind of throne on which a man sat with a silvery apeskin cloak around his shoulders, and next to him stood someone holding an object like an umbrella plaited from palm leaves or grass or both over him to protect him from the sun.

It was not fragments of speech I was hearing, I realized. It was the groaning of the rowers as they labored.

The giant heron cocked his head. He took one step, another, made sure that his shadow was not falling on the water, and stiffened. The ducks, on the other hand, drifted blandly, quacking, rocking, wagging their tails. The kingfisher had disappeared. Against the pale green background of the wild figs only the tree trunk fleet stood out, edging forward in painfully slow motion.

I began to get a cramp from lying so still and wished that the warriors, if that was what they were, would hurry up. Also I wanted to sneeze. I doubted that they would hear me so far across the water, but held out for safety's sake. If they were warriors and if they were hostile to us, then all would be up with us. And before I was caught – this I had vowed to myself – before I was caught I would snatch the stranger's dagger that he carried in a girdle around his waist and kill myself. Warriors or not, it looked like a show of force of some kind passing us on the way upriver. From where? Where to? It had been a long time since we had seen a village or one of the ruins, or cultivated lands with platforms on which boys sat making a great noise to scare away the swarms of red-beak finches, or herds of sanga cattle with their child herders, or women come to fetch water or to bathe sitting on flat rocks and scouring their soles with stones and joking and laughing boisterously.

We had long since left the beaten track of the gold and slave routes and followed a course determined by the stories of those seafarers and the desire to be the first to discover a shorter, easier way to their cities and open trade possibilities. The first to discover. To be first. At the forefront of innovation. First to return with an impressive report. What would we sell? Slaves? Ivory? Tortoiseshell? Gold? First find out, before anyone else, before all competitors, what commodities these people needed and what they could offer in exchange, and find out on the spot so that you could speak with authority and be the first to celebrate the victory of big easy profits. That was what it meant to play the discoverer.

I think the two of them had underestimated the game. It also seemed to me that they realized this but were absolutely refusing to acknowledge it. Now it was a matter of pushing on, pushing through. It was a fact that somewhere in the distance lay cities that carried on commerce. It was known that the earth was ultimately ringed around with water. One day, one day, suddenly, unexpectedly, there would loom up before our eyes a blueness which, as we approached, would grow distinct from the blue haziness of the sky and announce itself as a separate entity, as being composed of water, as being water, as being water in motion with waves with foam backs and splashing foam flakes. As being the water firmament on the edge of eternity. And we would hear a pounding and perhaps seabirds. And the last stretch we would all run.

Ah, how pleasant to meditate ahead, to listen, see, smell, feel ahead. To imagine experiences.

Our stock of food was diminishing and gave cause for concern. We grew dependent on the skill of the slaves and the knowledge of the wilds they had acquired as children to supplement our food. Thus, for example, they picked out a round orange fruit full of big pips with a thin layer of nice sweet flesh. And they picked out edible grubs: they pulled them off the leaves and pinched their heads off and baked what was left – which was not much – in the hot ashes.

I was imprudent enough to compliment them foolishly and long-windedly. I looked them boldly in the eye, created a relationship of familiarity, then cupped my hands and got a share of their fruit, berries, grubs, roots. Then I went and sat down with my gift halfway between them and the stranger and the eldest son. After a while the stranger came to join me and I gave him some of what I had. Then he shared his little with the eldest son. A complicated system. But the situation was not yet critical.

Funny incidents, like the time the eldest son caught a freshwater turtle and tried to roast it in the shell. It gave off such an intolerable stench that we all retired and no one would let it pass his lips, including the catcher and roaster.

Less amusing the incident with the sable antelope hit by lightning. Looking back I can in fact laugh bitterly. I can still see the stranger bringing out his elegant little dagger with the handle inlaid with jewels – emeralds and carnelians polished till they glittered – and trying to slice through the skin of the antelope's belly. He must have begun there because he thought the skin would be thinner in the groin.

Some distance away the slaves stood grimly looking on after unanimously deciding not to touch what seemed to us a lavish gift. A first sign of mutiny, perhaps? I don't know. The eldest son contributed by holding the antelope fast by the horns. The animal anyhow had no kick left in it. The stranger gave up the struggle. No one thought of looking for butchering equipment among the goods we were carrying. Or an axe or a spear or something of the kind.

The antelope's glassy eyes were looking at me wherever I circled around him, I thought fearfully. Perhaps the lightning bolt had merely stunned him. But no, he was really dead. We had chased pied crows away from him. These had not yet gone. They were hobbling about here self-righteously. Waiting. Waiting. Till the tedious human left. When I looked up I noticed a vulture in a treetop. The stranger gave a snort of laughter when I approached and asked why he did not look for equipment in the supplies.

Both he and the eldest son had from the very beginning pushed their weapons into one of the packs because it was too much trouble to keep them continually at hand. They were simply in the way. What prevented the slaves from overpowering the two of them, doing away with them, and making off? Were they then so unmanned? I thought I detected a glint in the slaves' eyes. They were watching like the crows were.

From the tiny slit the stranger had made with his dagger in the belly a slow dark fluid oozed on to the white hair. The air smelled wonderfully fresh after the rain. I wished we would leave. One could see a rainbow. There, far away at its foot slept the lightning. I wished a lightning flash would make the sable jump up and storm us.

Summer was starting to grow full and ripe. It was in winter that we had last seen the sea. Vague salty damp memory. Grown so used to this routine.

After an evening's consultation the two leaders decided we should cross the great river along whose bank we had been walking for a while now, so as not to lose our course yonder towards the sunset. Their joint fright at the prince or commander and his subjects or troops in the hollowed-out tree trunks had moderated the discord between them. This nearly flared up again when the stranger teasingly asked the eldest son whether he would be able to pick out a hissing tree for the building of a vessel.

Would you? asked the eldest son sullenly. Then they both laughed with embarrassment. Here, so far from home and hearth and from the sea, they sensed their relative powerlessness and saw only too well that they did not always have the situation under control. The eldest son slapped his calf with his cane, but listlessly, as if confessing impotence. I saw in their eyes that they did not know what to do. Men look so funny, like disappointed children, when they lose control of something but dare not openly acknowledge it. And I in my peculiar position as parasite hoped fervently that they would find a solution and get us shortly to those cities that were our ostensible goal. Every morning I blossomed at my most beautiful, for them to admire my orchid-like nature for its colorfulness. I gave no less attention to my appearance than in town. My private torments were increasing too. I was utterly dependent on him to whom I was joined by deeds of sale as well as (I hoped to myself) by affection. But utterly dependent like a parasite.

Time passed and the plan of crossing the river was not carried out. Neither of the two had the inner strength to stand up, call the slaves together, and track down a hissing tree and set to work. In spiritless silence we lingered on the nearside bank. The food supply was now rapidly becoming dangerously low, spurring the slaves to set game traps of raisinwood and one festive day to cook a bustard for us.

What I could not understand was that the leaders' obvious lack of resolve did not make the slaves think of quitting us. Every night they meekly allowed the eldest son to chain them together, a measure taken after the one with the money in his hair had escaped. Every night I would hear the rattle of their shackles as they turned over in their sleep. In the mornings the chains would be removed, and no longer neatly rolled up and stored away – no, they were simply thrown in a heap. It was as if we had all become dream beings in a transition to we knew not what. The days unfolded and closed again one after another.

The river remained a joy to the eye. We were in a place where there were saf-saf willows growing. The eldest son, or perhaps the stranger, had remembered that this was an indication of firmness underfoot should one wish to wade through the river. For such an undertaking we should most certainly have had to wait for winter, even the end of winter. I say so because one of the slaves was ordered to enter the water and see how deep it was. He walked unenthusiastically in till the water reached to below his armpits, then began to swim, and shortly thereafter we heard him cry out and saw the current bearing him along and fellow slaves of his running downstream to keep up with him, calling to him to struggle towards the bank. I saw his head bobbing further and further off on the surface of the water, and the further off the more it looked as if he were floating at his ease. Later his fellow slaves returned. Precisely where he drowned they could not say with certainty.

It was nice to observe the bee-eaters as they shot across the water after flying insects. The water itself was a brownish green and muscular, and lapped at the banks where rocks or tree stumps protruded. Of the willows only the tops stuck out. The limp branches hung half-drowned. I felt like the willows and let time flow through me. It was nice to hear the bush shrike whistle and never see him. We also grew accustomed to the cicadas.

The eldest son and the stranger recited poems to each other in solemn tones and asked each other riddles, me too, and once the eldest son sang in a wonderfully deep, rich voice. The stranger wanted to clap him on the shoulder in sincere admiration, but it was as if he did not like being touched, and jerked his shoulder away. He told of yearning for his bride. He called her name over and over like someone throwing a jewel from one hand to the other.

The stranger said: If the sky were now to smash down on us, we would scarcely make a dent in the turf.

He plucked a handful of lush grass from where he sat and chewed on it, and his eyes closed. He was dreaming. I put my arm around him. It no longer disturbed me that the eldest son could see our caresses. The slap of water soothed me like a refrain. I touched my ivory bracelet. Luck bringer. I kissed it. I had a swelling on my heel that was very painful, and of course mosquito bites all the time. What was that lonely bride left behind doing with her days where she sat without any tidings? What were people doing now in that city? Was there anyone besides the bride who remembered how we had departed?

Yet we did get to the far bank, and perfectly easily. A day's journey upstream we floated a roughly carpentered raft out from among the reeds and finch nests, and seeing that an island divided the river into two courses at this point, neither flowing so fatally strongly, we arrived without loss of life or goods first on the island and then on the far bank, where we spent a day to get everything properly in order, to inspect and check over everything. One of the slaves killed an oribi, throwing a knobkerrie that he had carved for himself during our halt from the light yellow wood of the bush willow. With this welcome addition to provisions the expedition once again got into its stride.

Our pace was quickened. There was a noticeable air of urgency about the two leaders, an alertness long last seen, as if they had undergone a personality change under the effect of the scrap of news about the city in the red desert retailed to us by the hungers. Both now walked at the head of the procession, each taking longer steps than the other, striding more smartly than the other; one even heard them laugh. Their good humor infected all of us. It encouraged industry among the slaves, who, dividing the work more readily in an atmosphere of co-operation rather than supervision, in no way fell behind their owners. We felt jointly attracted by that promised city at the foot of the rose quartz mountain.

Still, I could not help notice how untidy we looked. From above, from my litter, last of all in the line, I was struck by our slovenliness.

It could not be disguised that we looked dirty, worn down and shabby, dusty, our clothes full of fat stains. One of the slaves was no longer even carrying a pack on his head. How was that? What did he think he was doing here? Another had tied rattling round yellow seeds around his ankles that made suru-suru as he walked and one revealed himself to be a notable imitator of bird language, so that sometimes, after hesitating a while, birds whistled back to him in response to his call. It was funny to hear him talk.

I wonder how I looked to the other. A sorry sight but full of life at least?

How insignificant our little line of human beings among the tall rough grass stalks, a wholly inconspicuous phenomenon in the midst of frisking herds of zebras and wildebeest and redbuck, and the ever-amazed ostriches. We entered upon highlands where the air was fresher and the wind unceasingly bent the tops of the grass and bush and trees, a billowing in the grass, a jerky nodding from the bushes and a stately response from the trees. The loose hanging stems of creepers swung helplessly about. Their magenta trumpeter flowers peered tremulously yet archly from every level of the host tree. In these more open plains the clouds floated in the blue, independent of each other and came together only at odd times, as if called, to manufacture thunder and lightning and dissolve in rainshowers. We took shelter under trees and waited till they passed. It was colder here. We moved on, a shifting tableau through the days.

After the city in the distance which must be the intended city, which would have to satisfy all expectations, on which we pinned our hopes, for whose sake we exerted ourselves, mustered our forces, had reorganized ourselves, where we would find shelter, meet people, streets with people, buildings, markets, squares, windows full of smiling women, children in gardens.

The city – so said the hunters who had advised us to use the raft they had made for themselves from tree trunks and rushes and left lying among the reeds where the island divided the great river – the city lay swept by the wind in a red desert. Sunbaked red walls. And behind it on the horizon rose the rough jagged rosy peaks of the mountains.

And behind them? asked the stranger.

And behind them the sea.

Ah . . . The sea.

A slave had been the first to notice the hunters. We felt embarrassed that we could offer them so little in the way of food and drink. Actually they were better off than we were, as we soon noticed, and also much better organized. They were carrying their booty of elephant tusks back to their kraal and were in a hurry because they had been away longer than they had planned. Summer was marching on. The elephants, they explained, had migrated further than usual, thus they had had a long search for them, but patience and endurance had been rewarded. Contentedly they indicated the bundles of tusks. This raw form of ivory looked rather ugly to me, particularly the blunt ends cut out of the flesh, and the texture of the tusks did not look at all like what I wore on my arm. Yet it was claimed that the ivory of this region was of far higher quality than the ivory of elephants hunted beyond the sea from our city. How should I know?

The hunters were surprised to encounter a woman. One laughed so much that all his tooth stumps showed, and I got furiously annoyed and withdrew. In contrast our two leaders carried on a lively conversation with them. I understood that they wanted to gain as much information as possible, but I could not help feeling the hunters' stealthy glances on me. After a while I went and hid behind a bush. I heard the eldest son trying to arrange a barter and trying to buy provisions from them. I heard him take cross money out of his embossed leather bag with long soft tassels and let the coins tinkle through his fingers back into the bag; but the hunters were not interested in such a bargain, for, they explained, they had only enough meat for themselves. The eldest son had to put away his heavy cash with nothing achieved.

The stranger was more interested in the precise direction we should take. The city lay in the sunset, he learned. Still many plains, then the vegetation grew thinner, then the ground between the grass tufts turned to sand, then there was more sand and the tufts would quiver silvery here and there, then the sand would become dunes, they would loom steep and rippled, perfectly formed humps with perfect stillnesses in between, and behind dunes after dunes after dunes which we would wearily climb, there would lie the city.

But first the waters, said one of the hunters. Yes, confirmed another, first the waters, the great shining, profuse in flowers, profuse in shadows, profuse in game, the reflection that would seem to be a reality out of which tiger fish leapt viciously, where the honeybirds called one on without cease and at dusk the kudu stepped out of the mopani forests and the marabou storks flew up like ghosts to cover the moon with their wings.

Messages were communicated to the hunters to pass on, when they got back to their kraal, to the ivory traders from the city who would come and buy the tusks. Thus the stranger and the eldest son tried to restore a connection. I had nothing to say. The other slaves were silent too. We existed where we found ourselves at the moment, and they, the stranger and the eldest son, existed from the coastal city as far as here and further as far as the desert city and the other desired cities, and they existed even further than that, they existed as far as over the seas that lay between the lands, and in those lands too they existed. But I was without connection. I was solely I.

The hunters had barely disappeared from sight when the eldest son and the stranger leapt to work, filled with a feverish zeal that infected the slaves as well, and in a jiffy everything was ready and we could push on, after all the many days of drowsy bewitchment when we had been like sleepwalkers each spun into a cocoon of pleasant absent-mindedness. When the water spirit enchanted us and bound up our thoughts.

Secretly I was relieved that the hunters had left, for their lecherous glances felt as if they stuck to me, and I felt that I was struggling to pull the cloying streaks off me, from my breasts and nipples and from my belly; but worst was the feeling of ruttishness they had aroused in me.

Thus the summer moved on. The great river already lay far away, the city of our desires still in the remote distance.

One afternoon we halted at the foot of a koppie with a cornice of round rocks. We had by now several times come upon these koppies with tremendous rocks on top. In our coastal region we never saw such formations and we could not help remarking on them. It was almost as if we were discussing art works. We praised their proportion and splendid balance, as it were the craftsmanship and sensitivity with which they were so arranged that it looked as if they would have to roll down and rumble across the veld till they found a little hollow of rest where the sun could crack them open or perhaps till they smashed into another of their sort and splintered.

Now we wanted to examine such rocks from closer by and climbed the koppie, the eldest son, the stranger and I, while the slaves got supper together unsupervised and made our beds ready. The one who no longer carried anything was the one who gave the orders, I noticed. Strange that he, so unattractive, with his slight build and unremarkable features, had never seemed to me a potential leader, though I must add that till now I had never thought of possible leaders among them. They were simply the slaves, the eunuchs who did the hard work without getting any choice and obeyed the expedition's leaders without answering back. Could he possibly be of royal blood? One could easily get soppy in one's speculations. Perhaps he was simply the smartest of them: to judge by his organizational ability that was the most likely explanation. He wore a great white snail-shell about his neck. Still, I thought, he deserved to be watched closely: but I hesitated to express my suspicions to either the stranger or the eldest son.

Once I caught the slave leader opening a pack and taking tools out, adzes and gouges and awls and so forth, which had presumably been brought along to hollow out a tree trunk somewhere where that seemed necessary, a problem that had been surmounted by the use of the hunters' raft. I saw how lovingly he handled the tools, just like a craftsman. I saw him absorbed in arranging them in categories according to use and size, and saw how he then packed all the tools in again, very neatly, very skillfully. Then he put the pack down with the others.

There was a surprise for us on top of the koppie. Two surprises. The first was remnants, limited but nevertheless there, of stone walls of the same design we had encountered several times previously, only more badly destroyed, or longer in disuse. More dilapidated. No single length stood intact, there were only weathered knee-high fragments overgrown with thorn bushes; but one could infer the builders' plan from stone block to stone block. In the afternoon sun the stones shone with the same honey color as the blocks against which and over which they were packed. If one could have stayed longer one might have discovered other objects. Where had all the inhabitants gone? We wondered and guessed. Were their skeletons squatting under the earth of the plain around us, undecided whether to rise and brave the dangerous journey to the land of the ancestors, or did they feel abandoned by their descendants? No one left to make a libation. Only wine and hyena laughter. Here something was utterly annihilated. Here was nothing but sorrow, nothing but meaninglessness and battered traces of glory. From below a thin trail of smoke ascended into the sky in confirmation of our entirely superfluous presence. Ah, I sighed, how long are we still to journey?

The second surprise on top of the koppie made me even sadder. The stranger was the first to come upon a cave on the east side, but I was the first to notice the curious drawings on the rock walls. They seemed to look like people, but also like stick insects, painted aimlessly sometimes in a bunch, sometimes singly, sometimes one on top of another in rust-brown and white. Very faint. Who in the name of the creator of all things would have come here to immortalize himself, and in so unfinished a way? It was too odd. Surely not the inhabitants of the walled town. The stranger complained about the lack of finish and the obvious absence of artistic rules in these clumsy attempts. Obviously backward painters from a backward society. Totally amateurish. The work of adult children. Yet not quite. No explanation occurred to us. The little figures so free of all connection, exiled here in the heart of the wilderness. There were too many questions here, and the dreariness of no answers. Here people had come and gone, again come and gone, dreary, to all eternity.

Here, said the eldest son, is one that looks like a buck.

The stranger expatiated tastefully on paintings on parchment and silk that he had seen on his travels in other lands, the richness and subtlety of their use of color and the fine balance between the trees, birds and people – recognizable as trees, birds and people, he emphasized – painted by trained artists and classifiable in schools and trends, and valuable possessions too. With the blade of his dagger he scratched at one of the ridiculous drawings. Someone's way of passing the time, he decided. It has nothing to do with art. It records nothing, it does not mean to communicate anything, or to satisfy aesthetically. It is functionless. The more the stranger spoke, the more heated he grew about the rock drawings, and in fact now he began to scratch them off.

Here is something that looks like a woman, said the eldest son. It has breasts. Here is a snake, I think. And look here! An elephant with a scalloped back!

He went into an uncontrollable fit of laughter.

I turned my back on the two of them and stood in the mouth of the cave looking out over the darkening veld at the glimmering evening star. Far away I heard the voices of the slaves, but always against the noise of the wind, which sounded now louder, now softer, like breathing. I felt so depressed. I felt as if my throat were about to constrict, I felt as if the incomprehensible were about to choke me and I had to hurl a cry into the wind which would vanish in the wind.

It is all meaningless, I thought, and walked off and descended the koppie alone. I went as far as a jutting rock, and as I stood there I heard myself say something. Not say. Mumble. Stammer. I heard the words fall from my mouth in snatches over the cliff to be swallowed by the wind filled silence, words that spoke of a jackal that would run through the air with a burning tail and set all the air afire. So there sprang a jackal from my mouth. I heard myself prophesy feverishly of languages that yet slept, of strange trees that would one day march out through valleys and over hills and along the mountainsides.

I prophesied that there would be a walking around inside the earth. I prophesied that huge grey breakwaters would be thrown against the sea and that vessels would hide under the water and that there would be migrating back and forth and extermination over and again, and when it was all out of me, when all the fibrous sounds were off my tongue, I felt as if something had been gnawing at me, as if I had been gnawed full of holes and no longer obstructed the wind and had become without resistance; and afraid for myself I climbed down the last stretch as quickly as I could and hastened towards the slaves and the conviviality of the fire.

Once there, I asked them if by chance they had heard me. They stared at me stupidly and went on with their tasks. The one who no longer worked, the so-called leader, did not even look at me, did not deign to reply. Nor had the stranger and the eldest son heard me, it seemed, as I inferred after discreetly inquiring. I felt annoyed and very tired and not relieved.

Now it so happened that the stranger and I slept a short distance from the others near our own flickering fire, while the eldest son slept further away, though near the bearers and a big fire. After the sanga cattle disappeared watches had been set nightly. This practical measure had however lapsed and remained forgotten once we had been bewitched by the water spirit. The laxness of these times had certainly given way to enthusiasm and industry once we were on the near bank, but it was diligence that had required neither urging nor supervision. Even the chains had been left behind on the other bank, and the slaves slept free as we did. To tell the truth, they kept watch in turn over the sleepers on their own initiative, and over the ever-dwindling goods, and took decisions ever more independently. Of course their leader.

Now it so happened that the stranger and I never detected signs of conspiracy between the eldest son and the slaves; and yet one morning when we rubbed the sleep out of our eyes, both he and the whole bunch of slaves together with the goods were no longer there. Vanished. Completely. The stranger climbed a termitary and stared all around without success. The veld was simply veld, with veld-noises – a rustle, a twittering, a chirping.

We tried to track them, we urged each other on and had no success. We noticed flattened grass and footprints in the immediate vicinity of the fires, and that was all. We naturally assumed that if the eldest son and the slaves had decided to proceed with the expedition without us, they would have walked in the direction of the sinking sun, but that way too we detected nothing that looked to us like traces of people on foot. The hard earth showed no tracks and there were grass stalks askew everywhere. We wasted a day wandering about because we secretly hoped that they would come back. That did not happen. When darkness fell a great and horrible realization came upon us. We went to sleep in silence and rose the next morning in silence and set off walking at a reasonable pace. I must add that my sedan chair, the only one of three brought along from the city that was still in use, had been left behind. Without implements we could not chop it up for firewood and the useless object remained beside the ashes of the little fire for which we had gathered together the skeletons of brushwood, all in deathly silence.

We took our direction from the sun, but were forced by the course of rivers to diverge from it. Without slaves to carry us through the water we were helpless. We had no waterbags. We lived on the veld foods that quite by chance I had learned to pick out by keeping an eye on the bearers. It was hard work. I did my best, but we found barely enough to keep body and soul together. In our time of testing in this place of desolation we nevertheless felt of good heart and tender towards each other. But the terrific grandeur of the nights left us dejected.

One day, seeing vultures, we limped along to where they were circling. A revolting stench struck our nostrils. I knew we both had the same thought, but the stench was much too awful. Furthermore the vultures did not give way to us. They hobbled about the rib cage, presumably that of a wildebeest, and pecked each other. They ate greedily as if we, just outside their circle, did not exist at all.

We walked many days. The veld did not change. Sometimes we talked. I expressed my surprise at the eldest son.

They would kill him, take his money, and seek their freedom in the city in the desert – that was the stranger's opinion.

To this day I do not understand the eldest son's behavior, this foremost heir of the coastal city's most prosperous merchant who, because of his father's influence and power, had been given nothing but the best since childhood, nothing but the finest that civilization could offer, and who had become an eccentric, short-tempered dreamer and fantasizer who had taken out his bad temper on the helpless yet could also dispense alms lavishly. The last time I had seen this happen was on the outskirts of the city on the day of our departure. He took a handful of money out of his leather bag and hurled it from the raised level of his sedan chair at the leprous beggar sitting at the side of the road, without looking at the fellow. Some of the coins struck the man in his tense face. There was nothing for him to do but duck and then creep around after the money on all fours, since his feet were already too blunt to walk; and with hands deformed into dried-out mopani worms, as brown too, as grey and black, he tried to pick up the coins. To maneuver them up.

Rocking from side to side I disappeared around a corner. I think that outcast was the last city dweller on whom my gaze fell. Why don't the creatures drown themselves? They just keep rotting till they return to the earth. It made me feel sick. More than once we came upon suicides in the woods. We saw pairs of feet, some bare, some still shod in rough sandals, turning around at eye height or hanging motionless, and among the branches glimpsed the contorted faces of old women who looked as if they were hurling abuse at us. Outcasts too. Childless women, or women convicted of witchcraft and shunned because they could not prove they had not let loose the mysterious deaths among the cattle and caused the bad harvests.

Of course I often wonder how long a person keeps on till. Surely there must be a boundary somewhere that becomes clearer and clearer to you, towards which you then reach as towards the greyness of sleep and thence towards the grey dream in which, as in a smaller death, you meet good and evil, the inseparable pair, the twins who defy death.

My dreams fill me and help me eat time. It no longer matters to me that I cannot neatly dispose of time and store it away and preferably forget it; for now I perceive that dreaming and waking do not damn each other, but are extensions of each other and flow into each other, enrich each other, supplement each other, make each other bearable, and that my baobab is a dream come true, and when I see the little people I know they are dream figures that really hunt and really provide me with food and that they really see me but also do not see me because I exist in their dream, and they feed their dream by caring for me. We meet each other and know nothing of each other. We go our ways separately and depend on each other, they on me in that I am as I am, and I on them in that they act as they act.

Nowadays I laugh ruefully at my spasmodic attempts to use the black and green beads I picked up to measure what is so ridiculous to measure and record. I attribute it to my education, random but education nevertheless, in which division and counting and classification played such an important role as to inspire people to undertake a journey that ought to progress so and so, and bring in such and such, and therefore for this and that reason ought to be set about in this way and not another, in this season and not another, in this direction and not another, with this equipment and not that – in which every last factor was taken into account, and when the day of our departure arrived with late-summer laziness, when day slipped into the realm of night and we forgot our sleepiness and our yawns, when for a last time, purely out of habit, we looked at the sea and saw the dhows and the skiffs heaving and the sky begin to burn with colors of fire in the kudu-berry trees, none of us noticed that we were entering a dream. So treacherous are the adventures of sleep.

It is clear that when I have finished drinking this last gift of the little people I will gain entrance to a new kind of dream. The brew is unknown to me but I do not have to know it to know that crocodile brains are the main constituent. Perhaps that is what I have been expecting. Will a dark mumbling wind come and fetch me?

What will I do with the golden nails and the beads, with the near-black water pot and the ostrich eggshell, my possessions? I would like time to reclaim them. The nails were the most useless present. I could do nothing with them, and how to show gratitude for them remained a riddle to me. Here they lie in my palm like seed that might germinate advantageously.

Everything I do is discreetly watched, and even my last gesture, the lifting of the ostrich eggshell to my lips, will be observed and (hopefully, presumably, probably) approved of. I will do it respectfully, slowly and stately in a last vain effort to satisfy demands I do not understand.

But for them I would long ago have starved. I was in a precarious state when the meeting occurred.

Scorching sunshine early-winter, but I remained asleep in the belly of the great tree. I remained asleep from hunger exhaustion, delirious and slowly withering away, with too little strength to change my habitation, to move to better grazing, simply grateful for the roomy hiding place, bare and robbed of its foliage, uncomfortable colossus with its probing fingers. I remained lying half-asleep, half-awake, and did not know if what I heard was really taking place outside or was in my mind, for I became aware of people talking, but as in one's sleep they talked so that one understood nothing. These phantoms busied themselves around the tree and I wondered whether they would enter my own dream reality and bend over me. I smelled something. I smelled smoke. It frightened me. I was not prepared to believe I would be consumed in the flames of my delirium. Through the crevice I saw floating forms pass, and sat upright on one elbow. Smoke. Human voices. The phantoms carried long branches stripped bare and joined to one another in a rough way to resemble a ladder. I understood nothing of what was going on. Nothing of the events being played out around my dwelling. I saw faces. Through a haze of smoke and incomprehension I saw the ladder being leaned against the smooth trunk, men climbing up it with bouquets of burning twigs, I heard shouts of joy, I saw ghostly people dance, men and women and children, I saw them gorge themselves and lick their lips and heard them laugh, and I stepped out of the baobab, the meager remnants of me, stepped out of the shadow mouth of the opening into the blinding winter light, clad in the tatters of a silk robe, my eyes huge, my lips open, my hands stretched forward in helplessness. I spoke.

Only the next day must one or two of them have returned, for when I came back from my drinking-water stream there was a dry hollowed-out monkey-orange shell filled with honey waiting for me at the crevice opening. Dark brown, almost black honey with the coarseness of bee grub.

How to show thanks? I held the monkey orange in my outstretched hand and stood a short distance from the tree trunk so that I was easily visible. For a while I stood so. The bees in the disturbed nest above buzzed busily, hummed as they tried to repair the damage against the assault of the cold. In the movement of light and shadow it looked as if they were swimming around, falling and rising. Thus I paid tribute to the bees and to their accomplices.

Every day there was something waiting for me. When I went to drink water they came with their gifts and set them down before the opening. Out of curiosity I spied on them one day. I pretended to go into the river undergrowth but did not at once go to the water; I hid in the thicket and watched the vicinity of the baobab. I saw two men approach through the long grass. They were short, and the grass made them seem even smaller. They had a light skin color and short hair like lichen spread over the head. They had crude clothing and weapons. First they gazed at the tree, then quickly went nearer, put something down, and scampered off. The long grass swallowed them.

A ground hornbill came up, walking. I saw that he was heading for the baobab opening. I could clearly recognize the calculating look in his light-blue eyes, coquettishly veiled by stiff eyelashes, and I got cross, and before he could get to my present I burst out of my hiding place to chase him away. The next day nothing was brought to me. Only the day after that. Thus I learned to behave according to unknown laws, though I burned with curiosity and would have given anything to learn more.

Particularly welcome were the serviceable hide clothes that they gave me, with an eye to the premonitions of winter which was so much harsher here than the winters I was used to, harsher and drier and more yellow. The earth crumbled and turned to powder. The branches of deciduous trees showed confused silhouettes against a sky become much lighter. And the bauhinia flowers decayed into a frenzy of shooting seeds. Everything seemed to me as if abandoned. The ibis community looked dusty and untidy. Even the elephants looked dismal.

It affected me. Again a somberness came over me. The mischievousness of a mongoose, the water games of an otter failed to cheer me up. The head-wagging rock lizards did not divert me. I slouched aimlessly around.

Chased somewhere by the intimidation maneuver of a baboon sentry, I had picked up the first beads somewhere where a crack in the rocks turned into a crevice, somewhere in the dust among intertwined dry dead tubes of stalks, grass tassels, calices, petals, roots, somewhere not so long ago.

Humanware. Humans been here. An incalculable distance between me and those who had left behind beads and potsherds, irrecoverable time, unbridgeable estrangement, insuperable my loneness intensified by this small discovery, interminable the continuation of solitude, surrounded as I am by those who keep themselves apart and for whom I exist, but only as an apparition.

As an apparition I throve, became rounded and plump again from eating fungi and carrion flower stalks, python flesh, marulas, livelong berries, waterbuck liver. Whatever a winter and a summer had to offer to the eye and gathering bag and the bow and arrow of the little people, I too was fed on. There was no question of hardship any more, rather one of lazy overabundance.

Whom to thank, I sometimes ask myself. My water spirit is silent. So I thank the honey-bee. I thank the tree that houses him. I thank the earth that gives the tree its footing, with great difficulty, because it grows upside down. I thank the rain that descends to the very roots of the tree so that it can drink water and grow leaves and flowers. But the water spirit is silent. Baobab around whom the bees dance by day and around whose sensitive flowers unfolding like moons so many bats flap by night, in whose forks the rain pours rainwater for me, my water spirit is silent about you. Once I found an injured bat on the ground beside the daylight-filled crevice. At first I thought it was a funny flat frog shuffling backwards out there. Then I noticed it had fur. Then I saw the ears. And went down to the water. When I came back it was gone.

I searched the place where I had picked up those first beads. Continually, naggingly I searched.

The bat was gone. A necklace of ostrich eggshell fragments the color of wild pear blossoms and a handful of medlars were waiting for me.

Then latish one afternoon I discovered the pale knot of a rock fig in an overgrown cleft, and overhastily climbed the stone ridges, hauled myself up on loose hanging roots, and arrived on a small plateau. The steep side I had scrambled up was at an angle to both sunrise and sunset and offered a view across a long, virtually empty slope with clumps of trees. A few giraffes. The dust of a mixed herd of snorting, barking wildebeest and zebra. At the time I noticed nothing more. A flight of birds, yes, that too, swiftly dissolving into the distance. The wind was present everywhere. It rustled steadily as if it were the companion of silence. That was all I found in a thorough investigation of the plateau: wind and the background of wind, silence. I made believe this was the guardian who had wiped out everything, and woe to him who came sniffing around. Why scratch open, dig up, expose, reflect and deduce? Let be, just let be. Here there had been perhaps.

A city, perhaps, with ruler and subjects. I did not know what they came here to seek, what made them build their houses here of all places, with a view over endlessness, and whether they knew of the great sea that lapped around the horizons, and whether they imagined their various gods in the heavenly bodies or elsewhere, whether they observed ceremonies in their honor from which they departed, eyes glassy with faith and hearts full of good intentions, and whether they knew beforehand of their certain death. Or was death a game of chance to them, sometimes complicated by sicknesses, sometimes coming at a stroke, but in any event the actual beginning of life without the nuisance of a body and the time-consuming needs thereof, and if death is life, then they still live. Here. Right here.

The wind died down. In the unbelievable silence one of the big stones rolled down the cliffside, bouncing, leaping as if performing a trick, fantastic and soundless, and came to rest on the level below. The soundlessness gave me a fright. Now I no longer heard anything. Suddenly I knew that if I were now to speak, something tremendous would happen. The dead would arise, or no, they would become visible to me, and time would somersault, the earth would tilt, capsize, and hang upside down in the direction of limitless darkness and the spirit of the water would voyage into eternal space and forever be lost.

Then I felt something creeping in my ear. It tickled and itched and I shook my head. An ant. Something. An insect. I crushed it with my finger. And as if I had spent some time in a swoon, I now noticed that the sky had clouded over and that it was going to rain at any moment. Pell-mell I cleared out, possessed by fear and determined to get to the baobab before the lightning began to flash, but above all determined to be back in time in the time in which I belonged, for as I ran and sometimes stumbled too I felt behind my back another world growing, I felt that what had existed was extending its realm faster and faster, and felt that soon, in the very act of running, I would move in a wholly other time.

I reached the baobab with beating heart and a stabbing pain in the spleen that doubled me over, and I squatted in the opening and saw the rosette patterns that first raindrops make as they hit the dust.

So I yielded to the powers of my environment, or, to put it less despondently, I learned to live with them, as I learned to live with the veld and the animals and insects, with the choice of paths in reality and in my sleep, and with the presence of people who kept me apart. It is a strange experience to share a life without contact, and I often ask myself whether they are displaying charity towards me or bringing tribute. I try to behave fittingly. Acknowledge to myself that there is nothing for me to do but accept my fate as pampered captive and show myself grateful accordingly. It is as if the presence of others aggravates my loneliness, as if the distance between myself and other people has become greater now that they exist in tangible proximity. I see them walking in the distance, I see girls playing with a monkey orange, throwing it back and forth to each other, I see women carrying babies on their protruding buttocks, men with wrinkled stomachs and legs thin as sticks, all of them yellow as a tortoise's belly, and I hold my hand over my mouth to prevent myself from calling someone nearer. I hear the click sounds they utter, I mutter something to myself that sounds like the language of my childhood days. Words that had got lost take on dim shape. Mother I see before me, father, brothers, sisters. I see huts and very high trees with trunks pleated like billowing skirts and green foliage. Mother I see again. Warmth and softness, a slimness, long breasts with sturdy nipples. Voices I hear vaguely and other noises too, a chopping, a crackling. I remember suddenly dogs that never bark, and noisy apes, and there was gaiety, I remember, when meat was portioned out, ape-meat too, yes, and I had had a doll made of bark fiber, the doll had beads around its neck, the head was a club, and I had the doll with me when everyone fled from their huts into the dense underbrush, my mother yanked me by the arm but she was killed, her head was split open and I was jerked out of her grasp and driven into a knot with other women. There were a whole lot of male captives too. I held on to my doll. I kept it with me in my arms. We traveled and traveled and then came to a village. The male captives were herded together and something was done to them. Later we set off and traveled further and further and came to a city on a terribly big, immeasurably broad dam, blue from this end to the far end.

Now I have the name for everything: slave, castration, commerce, coastal city, sea, forced labor. Yes, now I have it all.

I have the name and I am not listened to. There is nothing I can do with the names. They are nothing but rattles.

Borne from far on the wind I hear the little people making music. The sounds seem to me like beetles jumping over a fire. Also I hear them singing and clapping their hands.

Now I will force a confrontation.

When they next come to pick baobab seeds to suck the sour white flesh off the stones, I vow – then. Then I will confront them naked. Then I will undress. I will lay aside my skin apron and my skin cloak with the spring hare bones, as well as the necklace of ostrich eggshell fragments, and I will confront them, challenging them, though with my challenge tempered with acquired grace, shy but queenly, seductive but aloof; and I will look them right in the eyes and force them to look right back at me and acknowledge me, as a human being and nothing more than a human being. That is all I am.

I did it. They approached talking among themselves, and I guessed they were coming to pick seeds as they had done a few days before. I took off the clothes, removed the necklaces, loosened the sandals from my feet and kicked them off, and before doubt and hesitation overcame me went and stood in the opening of the baobab. And they walked past, and up the same homemade ladder they had leaned against the trunk to get to the bee nest one of them now climbed, picked seeds and threw them down to his comrades on the ground, who nimbly caught them. Unconcernedly the picker then climbed down, carried the ladder around to the set it on the other side, and harvested there too. Then everyone walked off, each with a gathering bag on his back chock-full of the fruits of the tree.

I was deliberately not seen.

In this dream in which I am forced to live, I take refuge more often in the city of rose quartz, for thus have I already adapted the hunters' story. Not only does the mountain glitter rosily, but also that city in which I wander in the company of many others like myself. We do not have to talk to each other, we understand each other naturally. I notice the stranger there too, but detect no need for his companionship, for I am of a self-sufficient crystallinity, transmuted into pure bliss. I am one whole, and divided too and present in everything everywhere.

Strange that the water spirit sends me to a desert, but I understand, for, see, the water too has become quartz, everything has, stone and water and man have the consistency of quartz and the glory and the glorious knowledge of splintering and remaining glorious. Then when I awake, whether in the night or the day, I feel crinkled and stiff.

The insult of not being allowed to be human, that I have overcome. All ugly visions too, of hairy huts and skew door openings that try to entice me in and lock me up, all false solutions, all wrong exits; for I myself determine appearance and reality. I rule. I dream outwards and with the self-assurance of those who have long ago discerned that it is all just appearance I smile to myself, follow my own path diligently, will drink this parting poison gift in the nourishing awareness that dream leads to dream.

There is no other termination. That I concede. I am used up. To myself as well; but whether that makes up part of their deliberations is barely relevant, and why should they in their grief make room for the feelings of someone who let them down, who so lamentably failed where she should have been able to offer a way out?

Let the gods stare over our heads, the stranger once said. They know what they see.

That was precisely what I did not know. Wanted to join in. So I thought.

The stranger had stories to tell about many gods and religions, about the strange customs of priests and enthusiasts and prophets in the cities where he touched in the course of his trading voyages, and about their mutual malignancy and their competition for the blind obedience of the masses and their competition for the favor of the rulers, which could lead to being financed by the rulers, and the acquisition thereby of positions of power for the preaching castes, and all, all just because man feared death, all just to exorcise these fears. Promises of the cycle and promises of resurrection, promises of a paradisal hereafter, of the friendly community of ancestors, of salvation through abstinence but also through investment and bestowal; and every religion recruiting shamelessly and rejecting every other shamelessly.

And death a commonplace! the stranger said, and fell silent, and waited for someone to contradict him. Stories to scare children, was his conclusion. A bore at best, sometimes amusing, like adventure stories. Let us tell each other fables rather than try to rend each other over religion. Who believes me that there is a land where people ride on elephants? Who believes me that there is a land where people ride on an animal with two humps? Who believes me that there is a land where people yoke buffaloes on their ploughed lands, that there is a land where people use milk to make light? But you believe, you philosophers and manipulators, in paradise?

The stranger laughed scornfully.

There are enough wonderful things in life that arouse my curiosity. I am avaricious out of eagerness to know. Look!

He took off one of the necklaces he wore around his neck, a gold chain with a huge bloodstone pendant like a beetle on it, artfully engraved to look like a ladybird, only crueler and bigger.

Which of you believes that this jewel was stolen from the neck of a dead man who is still alive? he asked.

I can still remember the startled exclamations and gestures of aversion and the growls and the forced smiles on the faces of some of our foremost citizens, those who could not afford to display ignorance and so had to conceal it behind airy smartness.

I wish, sighed the stranger, I could travel to the outer limit of the world. I am so greedy.

I also remember that the eldest son was present on that occasion, and how he listened attentively and slapped his calf with his cane but as usual said nothing. My benefactor, too, seldom took part in conversations like this. Too sick. Too dazed by fever. My heart was with him and with the stranger. My benefactor's hand trembled when he slowly brought a spoonful of beans to his lips. What did he think of all the chatter about death, he who was touched by it? His eyes, deep in their sockets, betrayed nothing.

Of all the sorts of conversation carried on after his dinner parties, the ones that interested me least were those dealing with war. To be honest, when war was brought up I found a reason to dish up or clear the table or attend to something else of a domestic nature. There was talk of sea battles and of land battles, or armaments, piracy, of celebrated victories and the division of spoils, ransoms and extortion, raids, punitive expeditions and suchlike matters about which the men argued and tried to impress each other, and about which they could come out with the most divergent theses and get extremely spiteful and sarcastic about each other's theories. The supreme game of profit, that was what the stranger called war, and he was at least one of the few at the table who could speak from experience.

The little fleet of dhows under his command had already been on the attack and also been attacked by pirates. He had already, in contrast to the cityfolk, been in fierce combat with warriors. He had killed. Had himself been wounded. He knew what he was talking about when he referred to a bloody slaughter, for to him memories clung to such incidents and every battle meant more experience for him, cumulative knowledge of a reality with which, against his own wishes, he was professionally concerned, and not fiction. Not just stories of heroism. He had seen injured men tumble overboard, seen hacked-off limbs floating, blood and commotion in the water that attracted sharks from near and far, and had heard the wretched drowning men defend themselves roaring against the monsters' slashing bites, in vain. As calm and refined as he sat there talking, so barbaric the naked language he used. Chop, stab, mutilate, kick, stalk.

While the city folk, fat with prosperity in an uneasy peace on the edge of history, chattered about defense and building forts and ramparts, and simply chattered and did nothing out of laziness and envy and lack of mutual trust and above all out of stinginess, I suspected, and also because they themselves did not feel at all threatened. With the many dhows that came across the sea laden with wares they maintained excellent relations. Their own skiffs distributed the goods to smaller coastal towns and in exchange loaded leopard skins, ivory and ambergris, tortoiseshell and rhinoceros horn for shipment back to the coastal city and its wholesale merchants; and so long had this favorable arrangement lasted that they would not believe anyone who might predict a plot to ruin their flourishing trade. Who, after all, would be so stupid? It was to everyone's advantage. There was no question that these strange caravels that had latterly begun to call constituted any danger. Besides, relations had quickly been established with these newcomers. There was no question that they were capable of snuffing out a long-established trade. No, not these simpletons who had to beg for water and fresh meat and fruit.

To everyone, myself included, the stranger's reports sounded romantic rather than instructive and insightful. I took the heart-shaped palm fan and fanned myself. I nodded and smiled and passed a dish and made a witty remark and tried first with one guest, then with another, to shift the discussion into a lighter vein. I flirted and laughed naughtily and practiced my calling faultlessly. My benefactor looked satisfied. The scent of myrrh and the scent of rich foods, the scent of the multitudinous jasmine, the scent of the water I had washed myself with, the oil with which I had rubbed myself, the particularly complex composite aroma of civilization, that was what we breathed here. That was what the sultry city offered us.

That was how far my knowledge of warfare extended.

That it is innate in woman to have a spontaneous approach to atrocities, is a lie. Though I had already held death fast in my arms, though I had taken in my own hands a stillbirth strangled by the navel cord, and rolled it up in an old torn cloth like a parcel, and carried it off from our slave childbirth hut, though I had already heard sick people in delirium and heard the moans of slaves being punished, none of it has been of any help to me.

In the deepest, darkest, farthest corner of the baobab I hid. These screams, these war cries, this floodwater of fear dark over my head; this fear that cut through me, this bestial death rattle. I was cornered; like a rock rabbit in fear of death I trembled.

For days I did not dare go out. Then the stench of decay drove me out.

The wild rejoicing of the hyenas at night. I was too frightened to make a fire for myself in case it served as a beacon for those who had come to massacre. I crouched in the belly of the tree and understood the flickering train of thought in my baby who had chosen darkness over the light of life. It was an ecstasy of never being. It was the only true victory: neither death nor life had meaning. It was equilibrium. It was the perfection of non-being.

The stench drove me out. The fighting had raged nearly to the baobab, I could now see; for while I had been hiding both far and near had sounded the same, the same and everywhere, and I could not make out at all from what direction the attackers had come.

When the slaughter began, I caught a glimpse of the attackers. I had just started back from the stream, swaying along with the blackened waterpot on my head and my scoop, my ostrich eggshell, in one hand – that is to say, I imagined I saw someone, or more than one person, looking at me, and realized with fear, quietly walking on, that it was strange people staring, not the little people whose peeping, if I may call it that, was of unparalleled subtlety, in fact never noticeable. While these . . . Too clearly I felt eyes upon me, too clearly saw dark beings disappearing into the long grass. They must have been spies. And that same night. And it kept on. So long. The merest chance that I had a tree hiding place. Which they must not have observed and noted, for I was still quite a distance from it when I became aware of being pointedly watched. My self-trodden footpath seemed to me irritatingly long. With one eye on the tree I kept it in sight all the time. The distance between me and it refused to lessen though I lengthened my stride. There were spies. There were others here.

Others overwhelmed us. Who were these others? And from where? It is disheartening to remain spared.

On the day when I at last dared to investigate, I picked out among the gnawed corpses those of the little people. The other were bigger. I do not know how to assimilate horror.

How the scavengers must have feasted. There was too much for them to consume. The offering was too great.

Most remarkable the spectacle of one of the other up in a tree, stretched out over branches, the berries of the eyes already nearly pecked out, the fruit of mouth and tongue rubbled at. Decay that turns form fluid.

The ants went mad. There was far too much. They would never be able to break down everything and transport it fiber by fiber to their store places, where there would anyhow not be space enough. The ants scurried on all sides.

The bluebottle flies swarmed with delight over messed entrails, formed green patches like dangerous flowers, larger and larger grew the shiny flower, till suddenly the disc divided itself into multitudinous floating parts. These settled and caked together to make a new flower. They were everywhere.

The corpses had been torn apart by jackal and hyena and vulture and dragged far and wide and rearranged in an order that suited them; but everywhere bluebottles swarmed.

It was not possible to determine who had been the victor in the slaughter. I could pick up as many weapons as I wanted and build up an arsenal in my baobab. I could pack it full of ironware, feed it on iron to satiety, reinforce it with iron from within, install spears like staves in the opening.

I could not find out whether there were more corpses of the attackers lying around than of the little people. It was so quiet, aside from the usual birdsong and the breath of the wind, and in the late afternoon, as ever, unperturbed, the arrival of the elephants, their expert insertion of trunks in a row into the water, and leisurely bathing and sand-throwing and tranquil retreat with the oldest cow in the lead after everything had been achieved that they wanted to achieve. I greeted them.

First of all I went to fetch myself a load of wood. For now I wanted to make myself a huge fire. For I did not care in the slightest if I were seen or by whom. For even if the long grass were to bring forth just as many attackers again, I did not care. For let death come, let the death blow fall. For nothing mattered any more. For it was the end.

On the return trip, the long bundle of wood on my head, I heard a groan, or imagined I heard it. Or was I not imagining? I listened intently and heard nothing more. I concentrated, turned my head carefully away from the direction of the wind to catch the sound, and heard nothing. Remained standing there a long time, then went on and set the wood down in front of the opening. But I knew I had to go and track down the groaning. I had to track it down.

The knowledge drove me on. Carefully I inspected all the remains of people, and forced myself to do it systematically, to scrutinize systematically and to watch carefully for the slightest sign of life. I searched and searched and searched. I forgot about the stench and the flies and the vultures watching the spectacle from the trees and the horrible appearance of human beings destroyed, and searched over and over all around the tree as far as there was anything to be seen that looked like a human figure, human remnant, and I arrived at an ant-heap and again heard a groan. Now I searched feverishly all about, and further, and back again. There were interjections from a lourie, but I knew, I was convinced I had heard the groaning of a human being. It was as faint as could be, only just audible, only just. If I could only hear it again. Distance is deceptive.

I went back to the tree and drew a stick out of the bundle of wood. Using it I now searched around the anthill, poking with the stick in the tangled grass and dense ground cover; but what did I think I was actually doing? Was my sense of relation totally disturbed, that I imagined what I was searching for had shrunk to dwarf size, to fetus size – was that what I was searching for? Why was I churning around with the stick? I was searching for a groan, a groan without a body. A groan got lost here. That was what I was searching for. A groan had sounded in the air and I wanted it for myself.

Now I began to laugh. Half-sobs, half-laughs came from my throat. They came from my insides like moans. One after the other I forced them out like clods, and when they were out I felt like someone who had vomited. With my stick I returned to the baobab.

I made a fire. Spark. Flame. Fire. It flared high, for I threw more and more wood on it; I considered fetching even more, getting an immense fire going that would crowd out the smell of human death with the more pleasant smell of plant ash, and I also envisaged announcing my orphan presence via the fire. Let it be seen that I am. Let woodpecker and tapping beetle see it, let the leopard stay away from me, let kudu and duiker sniff fire and stay away, let what human beings remain see it and make up their minds. Do with me what you will. In godly impotence I walked among your corpses and achieved nothing, I whom nothing befell in the shelter of a tree, I who am not from here, do not belong here, do not want to be here. I heard your war cries, your child moans, your last sounds, and quietly remained in hiding, and when everything was over, stepped out of my baobab. Had eyes seen me?

Had they seen me shudder at what I saw?

If there are more of you, little or big, light or dark, come.

Gradually I got going again. It is winter again. Spent a summer, a winter, a summer, a winter here. Winter of hardship now, where I again have to rely on myself and have only the wind and now the phantoms too for company. White bones around the tree. The baobab clutches and claws at the sky. The grass stands pale and stiff. An aloe sucks the blood up out of the earth and wears it gaudily in a cluster of red knobs, splendid against the clear blue sky and only too attractive to the sugar birds. White skulls around the tree. Little by little the wind brings in dust to fill up the brain hollows and the pelvises.

I have to make new paths where skeletons block my way with their rib bones. I can do without the company of hyena and vulture.

Gradually going again.

A long time since I noticed baboons. Warthogs with upright tails often.

In fact gradually more and more slowly as if I were about to come to a halt. My territory contracts as my powers decrease. The humiliation of not being able to care for myself. Though I know what I can eat, I do not know how or where to look for it, and drift around again as I did right at the beginning; but resigned now. Why hysteria, after all? To what purpose fierce concentration? I let things go their course. On some days I find something, on others nothing. It does not matter.

There always remains the balm of the stream behind a ravelwork of lianas, its murmuring refreshment, the mood of coolness it creates, and there always remain the samango monkeys who announce their disapproval of my penetration with funny growls. In spite of all there is something familiar for me here. It has so happened.

The clattering stream and then the river into which it quietly and timidly debouches. The river runs towards where the sun and moon rise, towards where I once began to travel, towards the sea of the city from which we departed in search of a city on the sea at the other margin of the world.

I long for nothing any more.

Once, only once thus far, have I again undergone the pain of expectancy, when in the distance I saw a fire which developed into a veld fire that windingly sailed over the horizon and gradually devoured it. Fire snake, I earnestly willed, sail around me too and swallow me up. It continued to burn in the far distance and the smoke persisted as a pall in the air long after the flames had died. I got the smell of it, and I noted soot freckles on the bark of the tree.

Would whoever might be responsible for that destruction be aware of my nightly fire?

My answer is the poison that was set down for me one day during my customary trip to fetch water. Someone knows about me now. Someone has always known about me. But who? Here I can play a neat little game with my golden nails. I can count them out and simply accept what they say. Why not? I count them according to the rhyme. Ultimately useful, little nails that have joined together what was bygone and mysterious to me, precious little signs of a disappearing meaning. Now you help me to make my last moments amusing.

Good. I have counted them out and behold, the upshot is that I was not forgotten, which is as I thought all along. I will be thankful that my surmise agreed with chance. I no longer procrastinate. Recklessly I throw the nails up in the air. Let them fall where they will and lie and never rust. I was really a mistress and mother and goddess. Enough to make you laugh.

I stand before the crack and hold up in outstretched arm the last gift so as to be seen. Then I disappear into the dark interior.

Baobab, merciful one. My baobab.

I drink down my life. Quickly, water spirit. Let your envoy carry out his task swiftly.

Yes.

As a bird takes leave of a branch. Fruit falls. A bat. Like a bat, black and searching.

I dive into dark water and row with my wings toward the far side where in descending silence I am no longer able to help myself and deafly fly further and further. I will find rest in the upside-down. I fold my wings.

archipelago books

is a not-for-profit literary press devoted to
promoting cross-cultural exchange through innovative
classic and contemporary international literature
www.archipelagobooks.org